# CALLA LILIES, CURSES, & CRIMINALS

Lucia Kuhl

# Contents

# CHARACTER LIST

FAITH BRACKEN: Former Feng Shui Consultant to the rich and famous. Soon to be the owner of Feng Shui for Everyone and Abracadabra Floral and Flower Farm.

ARIE BRACKEN: Faith's brother. A detective on the Michiana Major Crimes Task Force and Nothing Fancy Garden Center owner.

TRIXIE BRACKEN: Faith and Arie's mother and Vito's wife.

VITO BRACKEN: Faith and Arie's father and Trixie's husband.

TIFFANY RICHMAN: Arie's daughter.

BLAKE BLOOM: Faith's current boyfriend and Arie, Pete, & Link's boss on the Task Force.

JENNA JASMINE: Arie's current girlfriend.

GRAMMA MONTAIGNE: Trixie's mother.

GRAMS BRACKEN: Vito's mother.

PETE: Arie's Partner and Monique Collins's fiancé.

LINK: Task Force member and Sydney Hovan's fiancé.

FRED: Black and white giant angora talking rabbit.

SAMPSON: Faith's chocolate lab pup.

LIBERTY: Arie's dog.

HUDSON: Tiffany's dog.

GRACE HOVAN: Owner of Grace's Rare Books, Sydney Hovan's mother, and Lois Collins's niece.

SYDNEY HOVAN: Owner of Moon Lake Dance. Faith's old friend.

ELLE COLLINS: Sydney Hovan's cousin

MONIQUE COLLINS: Famous Psychic and Sydney Hovan's cousin.

LOIS COLLINS: Sharpshooting matriarch of the Collins Family

LILY COLLINS: Meddling Spirit-Ghosts. Sydney Hovan's great-great-great-grandmother.

HOWARD CRANE: Eccentric fixture in Moon Lake.

MAX PETERSON: Faith's old boyfriend and boss in L.A.

UPTON CRESENT: Magician of Darkness. Brother of Crescent Homescaping's late owner.

TESSA JOHNSON: A friend of Faith's.

ALINKA ALBERTSON: Tessa's cousin.

RITA ROCCA: Tessa's younger sister.

KATLYN: Tessa's younger sister

JASON JOHNSON: Tessa, Rita, and Katlyn's father.

BLISTER: Master Computer Geek.

# CHAPTER 1

As I slipped back into my chair from the in-between, I couldn't believe my eyes or bad luck. Coming through the doorway of the half-full surgical waiting room were Special Agent Harvey Wallbanger and my ex-supervisor slash ex-boyfriend, Max Peterson. What horrible thoughts and deeds had I cast out into the world to summon those two? I was a good person trying my best to figure out a future with my family, helping my aging parents, and bringing prosperous and peaceful Chi into the lives of everyday folks. That was my goal anyhow, so what brought these two dregs into my world today? Worse yet, how did they find me?

Right now, I sat in a hospital waiting while my mother underwent brain surgery to remove a tumor. Mom isn't normal. She's a witch, and I suspect some kind of secret agent for a covert magical force of the U.S. Government. So, one wrong slip and who knew what magic spells her brain might unleash upon the world?

And why did I have to deal with Max and Harvey now?

The two advanced quickly. Both men were tall. Max was handsome and always impeccably dressed. Harvey had more of a weathered Columbo mixed with Longmire style going on, and he was a few steps ahead of Max. They didn't seem to be together. Based on Max's long stride and fast pace, I deduced he attempted to reach me first. Harvey, however, swerved to the right and cut Max off. Max stumbled a bit. Harvey's mouth curved into a slight smile. He liked people fearing him. It was there in the way he spread his shoulders and walked with a bit of a sway, taking up more space than he needed.

As for me, I couldn't move. Someone must have super glued my butt to the chair while my essence returned from the in-between. Arie, my cop brother, rose and blocked Harvey's access to me. Vito, my mob boss father, blocked my other side. Harvey would have to go through them to get to me. I'd taken care of myself for so long; I relished the sense of two formidable souls guarding my back. Since returning to Abracadabra, Arie and Vito's overprotectiveness rattled my nerves, but I welcomed their support right now.

"My mother is in surgery," my mouth said. At least it was working. Something about Harvey and Max arriving at the same time messed with my brain. "Whatever it is, Harvey, can't it wait?"

His head moved from side to side. Not a shake. More like 'Sorry, Sucker. I've got you now.'

"No. I'm afraid it cannot. We've got another body."

A man who I guessed was one of Vito's "contacts" moved from the corner to my brother's side.

Arie glanced at him. My brother wasn't used to a mob muscle as backup—except, of course, Dad. "And your point is? My sister didn't find the body. What does this have to do with Faith?"

Harvey spread his feet hip-width apart and crossed his arms. "That is correct. Your sister did not find her. But Faith is acquainted with her?"

Movement behind Harvey caught my attention. Max made silly faces from the opposite side of the room and waved his hands. At that moment, he reminded me of Horseshack from *Welcome Back Kotter*.

In response, a wave of coldness caused my shoulders to shake. I thought of all the people in my life. The fact that Harvey and Max were here... Had someone killed my nemesis at Crescent? Jeannie had done her vile best to make my time at Crescent as unpleasant as possible, but I didn't wish death upon her. Or maybe Lenora. The owner's wife. She'd always been a piece of work, but I didn't wish death upon her either. I may have fantasized about sticking a dead rat in her desk drawer a time or two or lacing her latte with laxative, but never death. And I only fantasized. I never took action.

My attention returned to the conversation. The men stared at me.

"Sorry, what?" I asked.

"Special Agent Wallbanger needs to leave," Arie said with his fists balled at his waist.

"Didn't I wish? But he'd just be back. Harvey always came back. He was like a boomerang Energizer Bunny, only more lethal.

"It's okay, Arie. Let him speak."

But Vito was quicker. "Let's move this conversation somewhere more private, shall we?

"Good thinking, Vito," I said, rubbing my temple. Somewhere in the Universe, a woodpecker attacked my brain. However, I didn't want to leave this room. What if the doctors came out?

Tiffany Richman, Arie's daughter and my niece, touched my arm. "It's okay. I'll stay here and come find you all if there's any news."

I understood what she meant. Probably because Tiffany was so young, she was the star of Magic School and the best of us at slipping into the in-between at will. Much to my overprotective brother's chagrin.

Arie and Vito kept me squashed between them as we walked outside and around to an outdoor area by a collection of ponds and waterfalls. Vito's "contact" stayed inside. I assumed to keep an eye on Tiffany.

Confident we were out of anyone's earshot, I stopped and looked Harvey in the eye. "Okay, Harvey, spit it out. Who is this dead person?"

His eyes narrowed, and his nose scrunched his glasses. "It's Special Agent Wallbanger."

"Nope." I dug my feet into the ground and crossed my arms. "No, it isn't. You are here interrupting my time in prayer for my mother, so it's Harvey. Now, who is the victim?"

"Alinka Albertson." He trained his eyes on my face, waiting for me to respond. Even if she were my best friend, I wasn't willing to give Harvey the pleasure of watching me react. Alinka Albertson. The name rang a bell, but a distant one. She was someone famous. Someone from the world I was entering as a witch. A vision formed of her on TV.

"The psychic astrologer. What does that have to do with me? I am aware of who she is from her shows, but not personally."

Harvey leaned a bit forward. "That's funny. You spent several days with her in the Bahamas."

Yeah, right, was my first thought, but something pulled at me. The bubbling of a nearby water fountain brought back the rolling cadence of waves crashing upon a beach. A memory of drinking lemonade on a boat with Alinka floated in the back of my recollection. Another of her dressed for an elegant but casual dinner hanging on the arm of the infamous Upton Crescent.

Upton, I wanted to forget. His older brother, Cash, was the owner of Crescent Homescaping, where I'd been employed until recently.

"Harvey." I used his name and watched him frown to buy me a few extra seconds. "You are obviously mistaken. I think I'd remember if I met Alinka Albertson."

His hands went to his hips. "So, you didn't meet her when you worked at Pharaoh's Pointe on Watchtower Island?"

Watchtower Island sounded familiar. "Jason Johnson's estate? I've never been to Watchtower Island. Crescent probably sent someone else. Cash Crescent and Jason were college roommates."

"So, you admit to knowing Jason Johnson?"

A haze fell upon me. My inner mind, the part that talked to what I thought of as the Universal Mind, had information it wanted to share with me, but I couldn't reach it. The haze was hard to explain. The experience mimicked driving in heavy fog. You're aware there's a house, a tree, or a mailbox, but you can't see it.

"Yes, I've met Jason at Crescent functions. We're both from Indiana, so we shared stories. I don't understand. What does Jason have to do with Alinka?"

Harvey stuck his head forward like a turkey. "So, you don't remember the murder of Brandon, the guard?"

His questions ignited my anxiety and frustration. Little twangs of panic grew in my chest while my shoulders tensed.

"What guard? I assure you, I have no idea what you are talking about." The woodpecker in my head caught a huge caffeine burst. The world spun.

# CHAPTER 2

I awoke to discover Arie standing over me in a room with bright lights, many cords, and beeping things. A beige and white striped curtain surrounded us.

"What happened? Mom?" My brain hammered the sides of my skull.

Arie leaned over me a smidge. "Mom is still in surgery. Special Agent Wallbanger barged into the waiting room and demanded to talk to you. We went outside, and he asked you about Alinka Alberston. He said they'd found another body. But Alinka isn't dead. She's in this hospital. She was beaten and left, but she's still holding on."

A picture of Harvey outside by the water fountains swirled in my head. "Right. I remember him asking. I don't know her."

"Well, he claims you spent some time with her at Pharaoh's Pointe on Watchtower Island."

Images flashed in my head. "Strange. You'd think two weeks in the Bahamas would have made an impression on me, but I don't remember anything but sand and waves."

The doctor came back into the room. "Your blood pressure is slightly elevated but not in danger. The rest of your vitals are good. From what your brother tells me, you've been through a lot recently—stress wrecks havoc on the body. I understand your mother is in surgery. Rest. Practice some deep breathing exercises and call your family doctor for an appointment. If you have any other problems, get back in here."

"Thank you, Doctor."

"I've got some paperwork to finish up, and then the nurse will be back to give you something for the headache and get your signature. Meanwhile, a man named Max stopped me on my way to your door. He wants to see you."

"Max, isn't he your ex-boss?" Arie asked.

"He is. Thank you, Doctor. I'll send Arie out to fetch him in a minute or two."

The doctor disappeared behind the curtain.

"Odd the timing of Wallbanger's questions and Max's appearance," Arie said.

I moved around in bed. I was still in my clothes. "Hand me my shoes, will you? And yes, I was thinking the same thing."

"Do you want me to send him in? And should I stay?"

I zipped my shoes shut. "Max knows you are a cop. He'll be intimidated by you. Send him in, but stay close. In case I scream."

A vision of Max and Upton breaking through my door flashed in my mind, sending a wave of pain into my forehead's center. Max had tried to hurt me. We hadn't talked at all once we'd gotten back to L.A.. In fact; I was sure we hadn't ridden back on the same plane.

The pangs of panic were back again. I grabbed the bed's railing. "Arie, I'm not joking. Stay close."

His eyes widened. "Are you afraid of him? If so, I'm not leaving." He planted his feet.

"I don't know. I shouldn't be. Just stay close."

"I'll be right outside the door. Yell."

"Got it, send him in."

I felt better. I had two shoes, was dressed, my hair had been finger-combed. Max came from behind the curtain. Max, like Arie, was a strikingly handsome guy. They could be cousins. Dark hair and eyes with chiseled cheekbones and a tall, athletic build. That's where the comparison stopped. Arie was forged from long hours and hard physical labor. He was who he was, and he apologized to no one for his character.He'd even changed his business name to Nothing Fancy, which described him more than the garden center.

On the other hand, Max was all about image, and he'd probably never gotten his nails dirty a day in his life. Max was who he needed to be based on the people around him. Arie was Arie, too often irritatingly so.

"Hey, Faith, it's great to see you." Max tried to kiss me on the cheek.

I pulled away. Not sure why. Something inside me forced me back.

"What do you want, Max?" I asked.

"Wow, Faith, you haven't changed."

"Did you expect me to?" I made sure to look him in the eyes.

He shook his head and sat in the chair facing the bed. I sat with both feet hanging off the mattress, waiting for the nurse to come in and release me.

Max's eyes softened. "No, not really. One of the things I admired about you is you were always you. You didn't sway with the breeze."

Okay, so maybe I was more like my brother than I cared to admit. Yikes.

"The nurse should be back with my paperwork any minute. Perhaps you should tell me why you are here." I looked at him. I mean, really studied Max. His black shirt was untucked, and he wore no cuff links. Black and white tennis shoes completed his look instead of his typical thousand-dollar loafers. His ubiquitous Crescent watch was not on his wrist.

"Did they fire you?" I asked.

"Not exactly." He handed me a slip of paper. "Look, this is the phone number you can reach me at. I know we don't have much time right now. Alinka Alberston was beaten last night, and Tessa and Rita were missing. I need your help."

There was Alinka's name again. "Am I supposed to know these people?"

He cocked his head and studied me for a beat. "Faith, I know you well enough. You really don't remember The Bahamas, do you? They wiped your memory."

I shook my head. "I can't say that I do. Who do you think wiped my memory?"

"Under normal circumstances, I'd say my male prowess would be offended, but we both know the answer."

Not quite sure that sentence made sense, but Max and male prowess didn't belong in the same sentence.

"What happened in the Bahama, Max?"

The nurse stuck her head inside the door. "I'll be back in five minutes."

Max rose. "Okay, give me a call when you get out of here. It's urgent. I need your help. I need it bad. We were friends once. And yes, you do know Tessa, Rita, and Alinka. Tessa and Rita are Jason Johnson's daughters, and Alinka is his niece. You and Tessa became friends when we were at Pharaoh's Pointe."

"So, if they are missing, why are you here and not on Watchtower Island?"

"Because the three came up missing in Moon Lake, and you are the only person who can work the magic of the Bluedorf Mask."

The nurse walked through the door. "Call me." Max mouthed and left the room.

# CHAPTER 3

"I can't believe you dated him," Arie said as we left my room. "He's pathetic. You couldn't find anything better with all the men in L.A.?"

Growing up, Arie seldom liked any of my boyfriends. There was one exception. He liked Alex Houston and even kept my secret. Usually, I would have taken offense at his comment, but Arie was right. Max was pitiful. He'd spent so many years as a chameleon he'd lost his core identity. I'd come to understand that our core identity supports our essence and grounds us to create a solid, stable persona.

I shrugged. "I was never in one place very long. Max was convenient. How much did you hear?" I asked as we turned a corner into a new hospital corridor.

"Enough. Do you really not remember?"

"No. It's as if my memories of the Bahamas are hidden behind thick painter's plastic sheeting. I can see something there, but it isn't defined. Frankly, I'm amazed Max asked for my help. I assumed he'd never speak to me again. Max and I had not spoken in the weeks between the time we returned from the Bahamas and my final day at the company before I left on my last trip."

"But you don't know what happened."

I shook my head. "Sadly, the trip is a blur."

"So, do you trust that you knew Jason Johnson's family?"

"Yea, Max's body language said he was telling the truth. I need to call Max and learn his version of what happened while we were on vacation. One thing I can tell you about Max is there is always his version and the truth. Sometimes those versions are miles apart."

We wound through a passageway toward the surgery waiting room.

"Can your superb body language skills determine when he is on point and when he is creating an alternate reality?"

"They can. That's how I managed to work at Crescent all those years. I could read them and stay out of the muck."

Arie held the door while I passed into the next corridor. "Do you know what he was talking about when he said you were the only one who could work the magic of the Mask of Bluedorf?"

A mask with giant feathers the size of a Native American headdress flashed in my memory and then faded to black. "I remember a mask. Jason kept it in a guarded room, behind a sealed room."

"So, you do remember being at Pharaoh's Pointe?"

Arie opened another door for me. We were outside the waiting room. "I think I was there. That's all I can say."

"Well, it's a start."

I stopped before we entered the waiting room. "I'm surprised you aren't working the case if Alinka was beaten in Moon Lake and Tessa and Rita are missing."

As I said their names, lightning-fast images flashed behind my eyes.

"Pete and Link are covering right now while Trixie is in surgery and Blake is recuperating. So far, Harvey hasn't fought them for jurisdiction. I texted Pete while listening to Max. They were not aware of the Moon Lake link."

"I see. Calling Max might help Pete and Link find her attackers and rescue Tessa and Rita." The more often I said their names, the more real the two women became. Almost as if I was pulling them to me.

"The longer someone is missing, the worse the odds. So, the sooner we tie this up, the better. Pete responded while Max was rambling. Tessa and Rita have not been reported missing. Technically, it's too soon to file a missing person's case, but with Alinka beaten, extenuating circumstances apply. I forwarded the info."

We joined Vito and Tiffany in the waiting room. Still no word. Which wasn't surprising. We weren't expecting Trixie to be out for at least another hour.

A part of me just wanted to forget about Max. I'd tried to leave all that stuff in L.A., but two women were missing. I couldn't do nothing. I grabbed my phone and walked outside, sitting my butt on a bird-dung-free bench.

The family could see me through the window. If I fainted again, or they needed me, we could connect in seconds. Max answered on the second ring.

"Faith, thanks for calling."

"I didn't feel like I had much choice. Put me on video and tell me what happened in the Bahamas."

"Okay," his face came on the screen. "You found the dead guy sticking out of the fence in Los Angeles. We left for Pharaoh's Pointe. During our first day, you met Tessa, Jason's oldest living child, Rita Rocca, the baby of the family, and Alinka Alberston, Jason's brother's daughter."

Another vision of me being very afraid of Upton and Max spun around me. They pounded on my door, and it broke. Fred and I hung on to the mask. And then I thought I killed Max and Upton, but my grandmother's ghosts said no.

But the Fred that was next to me wasn't Mr. Fred. He was another rabbit that looked like Mr. Fred, who I had owned as a child. What happened to the new Fred? Another scene flashed. I was outside on a beautiful patio. Tessa gave an emotion-laden Tarot reading while Alinka chanted, and Rita made snide remarks. Tessa warned Max he was in danger.

Upton was there. He made my skin crawl. Next, I saw Upton blocking my path and me trying to pass around him.

"Faith, are you listening to me?" Max asked.

"Sort of. Tessa told you danger surrounded you. Is that why you are here? Are you still in danger?"

"So, you do remember something?" Max said.

"Just flashes. Tell me why you need my help. Where's Jason? The police are investigating Alinka's beating."

"The police don't know Tessa and Rita are missing. Jason is still on Pharaoh's Pointe. Someone took the Mask of Bluedorf. He's dealing with the police. He's aware Alinka was hurt, but I've not informed him his daughters are missing."

Whoa, I did not want to be the one to tell him. The poor man had been through so much. Yes, he'd achieved fame and fortune, but he'd also suffered unspeakable loss.

"I still don't understand. How can I help? I know the detectives working the case. They are the best. What do you expect me to do that they can't?"

"Because Rita and Tessa's disappearance has to do with the theft of the mask, and you are the only person who can work its magic."

My muscles tightened, and my free hand fisted. "Max, you keep saying that," I said too loud. "What makes you believe I can work it? And why do you suspect the two crimes are related?"

"Because I know and because you about killed Upton and me with the mask? Now, will you help me or not?"

My lesser self told me I would regret not killing Upton with the power while I had it. Max was pathetic, as Arie had said, but at his core, and I mean deep where you had to dig for it, there was something lovable about Max.

"Max, I remember you and Upton trying to hurt me. Why should I help you? Tell the police Tessa and Rita are missing. And I don't know how I'm supposed to use the power of the Mask of Bluedorf if it's been stolen. I need to think."

"Faith, you can summon the mask."

"I have to process. I'll call you later." I hung up the phone. What was I supposed to do? Yell, "Here, Mask. Here, Mask." Or repeat a chant. Buy it a plane ticket. However, for a moment, I remembered power filling me as I held it and used its magic to protect Fred and myself and expel Upton and Max. Why did I need to get rid of Max?

# CHAPTER 4

The entire time I'd been talking to Max, Grams Bracken and Gramma Montaigne's ghosts had been standing in front of me with their arms folded across their bodies and tapping their toes.

After I ended the call with Max, I left my phone to my ear. At least with my phone out, people wouldn't think I was talking to myself. They had mental wards here at this hospital. I'd already landed in the ER. Didn't need to be a patient on another floor.

"You two have some explaining to do," I said to them. "I remember riding in a motorcycle sidecar powered by two brooms petting a lifeless rabbit that looked like Mr. Fred on my lap. My next memory is lying in a hammock between two cedar trees on an island floating above Moon Lake. I recognized the view location as Moon Lake because I could see The Collins Spread from one side and The Bear from the other. You two kept making me drink this awful tasting foaming aqua liquid."

A man neared me. His eyes grew wide. "That was a great movie," I said, so he wouldn't call the authorities.

Gramma Montaigne's ghost sat on the bench opposite me. "I guess we are busted. Look, we don't have a lot of time. And we were going to tell you when you'd gotten further along in your magic training. It's all a long story, but you do possess the power to work the mask. Jason Johnson is family, as are his daughters. So, no matter what you think of Max, you need to help get them back."

"What about the police?" Okay, my comment sounded whiny, but right now, all sorts of jumbled visions raced through my head, so I really didn't care.

"Because magic is in play here and old curses and protections. The police aren't trained in magic and aren't in touch with their powers. And yes, both Detectives Pete and Link are engaged to women who possess magic, but the guys' powers are still buried."

"Wow, I don't know. I've had a serial killer on my path. Look at all the people who have died around me. How many more times can I go through whatever I went through at Pharaoh's Pointe before I'm toast? I want to open The Magic Factory and my businesses. If I help, will there be anything left of me?"

Grams Bracken's ghost huffed. I didn't know ghosts could do that. "First, toast is a bread you put in the toaster. That's a stupid saying. Faith, you are needed for things we don't have time to discuss right now."

"See, that's the problem. We never have time. All you ever do is dole out small pieces of information. I'm a big picture kind of girl."

"If we told you everything at once, you'd be so overwhelmed you wouldn't know what to do."

I switched the phone to my other ear and fidgeted on the bench. Sitting wasn't my thing anymore. I'd gotten used to moving around. Life had been so less complicated before I found the first body.

"Really! And you don't think I'm overwhelmed now? I've had a serial killer in front of me for months, and people have been dying around me. Do I want to step further into the abyss? Doesn't sound like a smart move to me."

"Enough with the serial killer and people dying. Quit whining and pay attention. You always were a stubborn child," Grams said.

"I learned from the best."

"I'll ignore that comment. If things had been different, Alex Houston would still be in prison, and Lizzie Raymont would be in jail for the murder of her father. Magic helped you clear them both," Grams said.

Gramma Montaigne took over. "Faith, you are just getting started. And the first stages of magic are hard. But it'll get easier, and you'll start to see all the wonder you can add to the world. But first, you wade hip-deep through the manure, and for a period, you are struggling in a football-sized field of poo."

"I shoveled enough horse poop in my youth. Manure, I can handle. Magic, not so sure."

"Princess," I heard Trixie's faint voice say from the in-between. "Stop being so darn difficult. I've devoted my life and missed most of yours to rid the world of dark energy. Now, more than ever, the world needs us. My minutes may be numbered. I should have sprinkled more magic dust before they started the operation. One thing you need to know, magic isn't easy. Magic is complicated and often backfires until you perfect your skills. It sucks magic can be used for evil as well as good. But, and this is a big but, when you actively train and strive to master your powers and use them for the benefit of others, there's no higher high. I've got to get back. Got to keep an eye on my surgeon. Don't want him to miss. He's here, Faith."

Her presence disappeared.

"Okay, tell me one thing. I remember I had to protect myself from Upton in the Bahamas. Max was with him. How do I know this isn't a ploy for them to come for me again?"

Grams sighed. "Arie is right. Max is pathetic, but he loves Tessa. He hasn't admitted it yet. His personality has changed so many times he doesn't remember himself when he looks in the mirror, but Tessa has impacted Max, and his magical self understands he needs you, and he needs Tessa to find himself."

Gramma Montaigne interrupted Grams Bracken. "Max is the person he's always been looking for. We all are the people we've always been searching for."

"If that was supposed to make sense, I've got news for you. It didn't," I said. Actually, it sort of did. But right now, I didn't want to give them the satisfaction.

"Are you going to tell me how to find this elusive mask and work it?"

They looked at each other like the joke was on me.

And then I remembered talking to the police detective. "Wait. Wasn't it already stolen once? And didn't you two give it to me to use to defend myself? You two stole the mask."

Grams shrugged. "It comes and goes. It will find you when the time is right, and you'll know what to do. But this time, the process will be more complex."

They disappeared. Of course, it would be more complex. Why would magic ever be easy? Because if it were easy, it would be used for evil. The theory I'd been given was that those looking to use magic for darker motives wouldn't put in the effort required to learn and would probably blow themselves to smithereens. Based on the darkness reported by the media, I'd say many people put in the work.

# CHAPTER 5

When I put my phone away, I sensed Vito behind me. "Vito, how long have you been listening?"

"Long enough. Nice touch with the phone. Glad a few of my tricks have rubbed off on you." He sat on the bench across from me. "Arie told me about Max and Jason Johnson's niece and daughters. Have you come to a decision?"

"I'm thinking about it."

"Thinking is not choosing."

I grimaced.

"That face will only give you ugly wrinkles. I may not have been there as a father figure, but I'm here now, and I've learned a few things on my loops around the sun. One of them is thinking rarely accomplishes anything. Deciding makes things happen. Second, magic like music and all things creative can't be fought. They refuse to be ignored. Ignoring them will only make your life unfulfilled."

What was today? Wisdom Day. I didn't want wisdom. If my brain wanted to explore whatever happened in the Bahamas, it would show me the whole picture instead of a jumbled jigsaw of hazy memories. But two women were missing, and one was fighting for her life. I needed to stop whining, pull on my big girl britches, and do whatever it took to help find Rita and Tessa. But whining required less energy than action.

"I've followed my creativity and the Chi forever. Isn't that enough? I'm tired of the destruction that seems to be the magic's path."

"If it were enough, you wouldn't be asked to walk the path, and the path isn't always this hard. Once the gunk clears away, magic can be wonderful."

"Then why did you and Trixie stay away for so long?"

He bowed his head for a minute. I hadn't meant to say that. It slipped out. Apparently, I still hadn't worked through all my stuff.

"It was a different time, and when we were ready to come back, we discovered we'd raised our children to be as stubborn and pigheaded as we were."

I brushed a tear from my eyes and batted another. "Okay, well, that may be true; however, back to the question at hand. I don't even know where to start helping. Pete and Link are dedicated, experienced cops, and I'm sure Arie will join the investigation. Blake is probably involved in some capacity, so what can I add?"

"Well, what if we worked as partners? The landscape could run without me for a few more hours. Able, or rather as you and Trixie call him, The Peacock thinks he owns the place. He can strut a little prouder, acting as the boss for a while."

"Why do you keep him around?" I asked to change the subject.

Vito shrugged. "He's a good designer, and his bravado provides comic relief."

I rolled my eyes. There was nothing funny about The Peacock's high estimation of himself.

But then, people at Crescent had called me Feng Shui Witch because they assumed I thought I was the cat's meow. When really, I tried to keep my head down and do my job. Not get mired in the muck.

I was stalling. Why was the decision to help Max so tricky for me? Of course, I wanted to find Tessa and Rita. Jason had been nothing but kind to me. He'd be frantic as soon as he found out they were missing.

So, what was in my way? I didn't want to deal with another investigation. I'd already done too many. I wanted to focus my energy on opening The Magic Factory, The Flower Farm, and Feng Shui for Everyone.

"Okay, I'll ring Max and tell him we are on the case."

"Vito smirked. Don't tell him we are on the case. Let's keep Max guessing. It will do him some good. Daughter, how in the world did you get involved with that man? His essence is so thin a fairy could blow his soul away."

I pushed my hair behind my right shoulder. "Man, you guys are critics. You've never liked any of my boyfriends."

"Not true. I liked Alex Houston until you started dating him. He was too old."

I rolled my eyes. Vito laughed.

"I like Blake. He's a keeper."

My phone rang. The new number I'd put in for Max lit up. "It's Max."

"Get as much info from him as you can without letting on we are taking the case."

I swiped and put Max on speaker. "Hi, Max. I haven't made any decisions yet, but before I can, I need some info."

"Okay, shoot."

Who was I kidding? Max knew me well enough to know I'd take the case. He knew it before he came to me. Max never did anything without calculating how the outcome would play for Max. And when he said. "Okay, shoot." He was aware he'd won. Whatever.

"Okay, for starters. What was Alinka doing in the area, and where exactly did Tessa and Rita disappear from?"

"Rita came to town to participate in a month-long writing retreat taught by Elle Collins. I know you and Elle are friends. You talked about her over the years."

"So that explains Rita. What was Tessa doing here?"

"You sound like you own this area. The California Girl is all gone."

"She was never there, Max. The Indiana Girl tried to be something she wasn't." As I said the words, a chill came over me. They were true. I had wandered all those years. But I wouldn't change a second.

He grumbled. "Anyway, Rita called Alinka and told Alinka she believed she'd seen Katlyn, who is Rita's older sister and Tessa's younger sister. Katlyn ran away years ago when Katlyn was only seventeen. Rita thought she saw Katlyn working in Moon Lake."

"Okay, go on."

"Because of Rita's call, Alinka came into town as a last-minute participant in a Psychic Symposium Monique Collins is holding this week. Alinka also saw and talked to Katlyn. Although, according to Alinka, Katlyn denied her identity. So Tessa boarded a plane, and since she was coming here without daddy, I decided to meet her." He paused.

"So why didn't Jason come to town?"

"Because no one told Jason. Tessa said they didn't want to get his hopes up."

"Go on."

"When I got to our inn, all that remained in the room was a bag of bones and Tessa's and Rita's phones." My hands shook on the word bones. Max continued. "A few hours after I arrived at the hotel, the authorities found Alinka's body behind a bar by a dumpster near South Bend Regional Airport."

"How'd you find out? Why did the authorities connect you?"

"They didn't. The cops called Jason, and Jason sent Tessa a text. I read it on her phone."

"So you haven't talked to the police."

"No. I was hoping you'd help me talk to your brother."

"How'd you find me here?"

"I stopped at Nothing Fancy. As I walked in, someone asked the young girl behind the counter if they'd heard anything about Trixie's surgery. I remembered your mother's name and listened to the rest of the conversation. Figured you'd be here."

"Wow, I'm impressed. Quality detective work. I'll put you in touch with my brother's partner, Pete."

Vito looked over my shoulder. His smile changed to a frown.

"I've got to go. Something isn't right with my mother."

"Good luck," Max said as I hit the end button.

"What's up?" I asked Vito.

"Arie's waving us in. His expression."

Dread filled my soul.

# CHAPTER 6

"What's wrong?" I asked as we reached Arie. "The nurse came out a minute ago. There are complications. Trixie pushed off the breathing mask, screaming for her magic dust and yelling, 'he's here.' They can't calm her down."

"OMG, I thought she meant the doctor. I goofed," I said. Leaning against a big cement decorative sphere for support, I slipped into the in-between.

"Faith, don't do it. Let me," I heard Vito say from a far-off place.

My essence was already in the room. "Faith, the corner," Trixie yelled. "Magic dust." The staff tried to restrain Trixie, but she fought them off. "Throw your dust."

I pictured the magic dust in my purse. I saw my hand reach into it and grab the dust pouch. I yanked it into the room.

"What the heck?" A nurse said. "Where'd that flying black velvet bag come from? What's going on?" They all backed away.

"Faith, fire away. I'll run the spell," Trixie said. "Vito, get out of here. This is a woman's job."

The massive formless evil in the corner advanced on Trixie and me. I concentrated on hitting its center mass.

"Go for the throat area," Vito said.

"I can't find it."

"Just above where its chest should be."

I tossed. Trixie recited a bunch of syllables I didn't understand. The staff huddled tightly in the corner. The magic dust flew like a twinkling sword across the room.

"Do you see that?" A guy in scrubs whispered.

"I see it, but I don't think we should ever mention it. Somebody stop the video." The man I recognized as Trixie's surgeon ordered.

The arrow hit the darkness, and it exploded in a blaze of red, fireless flames. Trixie's beeping monitor alarms pierced the silence.

Vito sprayed the room with dust. "Faith, we have to go and let them work."

"Why? They don't know we are here."

"On some level, they do. We've just scared the living breath out of them. They need us out of here."

We slipped back into our bodies. I clutched the cement sphere thing for support while readjusting to my body.

"Trixie came to me while I was talking to Grams. She said 'she wished she had her magic dust. He was here.' I should have taken it to her. This magic stuff is so complicated."

Vito placed his arm around my waist and led Arie and me back inside. "If Trixie had wanted you to bring her magic dust, she would have told you. Your mother is not one to hold her tongue. She has never been, nor will she ever be. It isn't a part of her nature."

We returned to the waiting room and huddled in the corner. "You let Faith go, but you wouldn't let me," Tiffany said to Arie.

"A, your aunt is older than you, and B, I didn't let her go. She went before we had a chance to stop her."

"So, that's the answer. Be quicker on the draw than you can speak."

"Try it, Youngster, and you'll be on dish duty for the rest of your life. Tonight, Faith has dish duty."

I relaxed into my chair's back. "So it looks like we'll be eating at Starr's Saloon tonight."

"How's Grams?" Tiffany asked.

I shrugged. "The threat is neutralized, and more magic dust has been spread. Maybe we should pop in every hour and replenish the supply."

"Not a bad idea," Vito added.

I needed to talk to Gramma Montaigne again, and I needed to use the bathroom. Like now. "I'm going to the ladies' room. I'll be right back."

Vito looked up at me. "Do not stray," which was Vito's way of saying, 'DO NOT go back into Trixie's room.' I had to admit it was weird at fifty taking orders from your parents, but they were the experts on all things magic, and Arie, Tiff, and I were newborns.

I wandered until I found the nearest bathroom and checked all the stalls. I was alone. "Gramma, did I cause Trixie's complications? Did my indecision? What was that thing in her room?"

Gramma Montaigne sat atop the stall walls. "It was a Murker's demon outside of human form. They fill the soul with darkness, hate, and anger. When they are in human form, they use words and gossip as their primary weapon. It knew Trixie was strong, so it had to attack her when she was in a weakened state, and it was outside of a body for added energy. No, you did not cause the incident?"

"Will it go back inside a body, or does that one always exist outside the body?"

She shrugged. I wanted to call her on that shrug. As a kid, she yelled at me hundreds of times for that very same action. "It's hard to say. Some hop from body to body. Some have their own, and some never take a body. It tried to attack because of Trixie's unconscious state. It didn't count on her calling for reinforcements."

"Will it come back?"

"At some point? But you fried it pretty bad. It'll take it at least a week to regroup."

I wanted to ask if Trixie would be alright. But what if I didn't like the answer? I'd just gotten her back—more back than in any time from my childhood. I didn't want to lose her now.

"We Montaigne women don't go down without a fight, Faith. Trixie still has a lot of work she needs to do."

The door opened, and someone entered. Grams disappeared.

# CHAPTER 7

An hour later, they summoned us into the room where they gave you the good or bad news. Tiff held my hand so tight it turned red. As we sat, Vito placed his palm on my arm.

We'd been in the room about ten minutes when the surgeon crept in wearing a deer in headlights look.

"After the complications ah, umm settled down, we were able to remove the entire mass. Trixie was under a long time, so she'll be in recovery for several hours. Professionally, I'd say the chances of a full recovery were diminished by her advanced age and the size of the mass. However, in my opinion, Trixie is one tough, stubborn, old broad whose willpower overrides logic. I think she'll be fine."

Tears wet my eyes while the tightness in my muscles dissolved. I exhaled and then laughed. The surgeon had expertly described my mother.

"Sorry about any trouble she caused," Vito said. "My wife does things on her own terms."

The surgeon shook his head. "That's what makes her special. And the only way to go through life. Why don't you all get something to eat and check your messages? You can see her this evening when she goes into a room."

"Okay, thank you," I said.

"Oh, as the mask came off, she mumbled something about telling her family she was taking the magic dust into recovery. Not to worry."

"Good to know," Arie said. We watched the surgeon disappear, shaking his head. "I'd like to be a fly on the way in the staff breakroom about now."

Vito laughed out loud. "And the surgeon thought I was scary."

Arie dragged his keys from the front pocket of his jeans. "Okay, since we are done terrorizing the hospital staff, Tiff and I need to run an errand regarding her parents' estate. And then we'll be back."

"I better check in at the Nursery. And I'll stop by and let Sampson out for you, Faith. Don't want Able thinking he can run the place without me," Vito said. "I'll be back in ninety minutes."

I grabbed my purse. "I'm going to get a burger downstairs, and then I'll slip in and check on the magic dust level before going up to see Blake."

Vito patted my arm. "Check, but don't get in the way. They may not be able to see you, but they'll feel you on some level."

I leaned down and kissed him on the cheek. "Yes, Father."

"When we all get back, we can tackle the magic side of our magical missing person case."

"So we are taking the case?" Arie said.

"Son, I'll fill you in when we return."

I rode the elevator down to the basement, ordered a cheeseburger from the cafeteria, and carried my tray outside to eat on the patio. Their burgers weren't quite as tasty as Candy's in Abracadabra, but close. And the view of the ponds, the fountains, and the prairie grasses was soothing. Much better than the hardness of the concrete walls and tile floors. The plants and light inside helped the Chi, but there was only so much flora could do.

My phone's ringing interrupted the melody of the flowing water and swaying grass in the breeze. Blake's name popped on my screen. Joy flooded my heart. I turned in my chair to face the corner. It felt more private and provided a better signal.

"Hey, beautiful. Any word on Trixie?"

"She's in recovery. I'm finishing up a burger, and then I'm coming upstairs to see you."

"I see. So your stomach was more important than your boyfriend."

"My boyfriend. You mean the guy I'm having lunch with, or you?"

"Very funny. Take your time. I'll be here. Although, they are letting me out of here tomorrow on good behavior."

"I doubt it's because you've been good. The administration wants to get rid of you because you've been hogging the cute nurses' time."

"That too. See you in a few."

I turned back around and noticed a plastic bag on my table. My phone dropped from my hand. Inside the bag were bones and a card with my picture on it. On the flipside was a photo of Alinka Albertson by the bear statue in Moon Lake and pictures of Tessa and Rita entering The Inn near Plymouth. The serial killer was here in the area. My hometown. In this hospital. Was the serial killer the darkness I'd fought in Trixie's room? Pulling my magic dust from my purse, I sprinkled it over my head and around myself, dumped my tray, and decided to slip into the in-between. I had to make sure Trixie was protected. And I had to call Arie and get human protection for her. I sent Arie a text and slipped into Trixie's room.

Vito beat me to it. His dust contained more gold sparkle than mine. Trixie's dust had more silver. Every inch of Trixie's recovery room shimmered in gold and silver dust. Despite all their divorces, I knew my father loved my mother, but this room was breathtaking. I only hoped someday Blake would love me this much.

"Get your butt into Blake's room now." Arie's reply message read. Vito's contacts are in the hospital and will guard the door.

# CHAPTER 8

As soon as I cleared the entrance to Blake's room, two big men in dark suits and glasses closed the door. I could see the tops of their heads through the window.

"It's okay," Blake said as he reached for my hand. "Arie sent me a text and filled me in. Faith, sit down, take a few deep breaths. Tell me what happened in any order you need. Tell me about the Bahamas. The bones downstairs. Whatever comes out first. Spit it out." His hand rubbed across my back. I sat on the bed and inhaled a couple of deep breaths.

Where did I start? There was so much.

"Okay, I sat outside by the fountains. I turned toward the corner to get a better signal while we talked. When I turned back around, these were on the table." I pulled the bag from my pocket and handed it to him. Blake grabbed a tissue, took the bag from me, and laid it on the bedside table.

"Aren't you going to look at it?"

"I will, but first, tell me the rest."

"Well, you should look at it. The serial killer has Tessa Johnson and Rita Rocca. Alinka Alberston's cousins who were raised as sisters."

"How do you know that?" Blake asked.

"How do I know that? Do you know that Alinka is in this hospital? She was badly beaten and is clinging to life. Harvey came to ask me questions about her. She was beaten in Moon Lake and left for dead behind a bar out by the airport." The words spilled out.

"I'm aware they found her body. How do you know she was beaten in Moon Lake?"

"I just do. So flow with me here. I need to back up."

"Okay, tell me however you can." He was almost always so sweet. A world apart from Max. I must have been really desperate when I dated Max. Really desperate. Anyhow.

"I was in the waiting room this morning. Special Agent Harvey Wallbanger walked in, and a few steps behind him was my ex-boss slash boyfriend, Max."

"Max, the guy you went to the Bahamas with?"

"Right. One and the same. Harvey told me Alinka had been killed and wanted to know what I knew. At the time, I didn't know anything because I didn't remember meeting Alinka or being at her uncle's spread on Watchtower Island." My mouth was having trouble keeping up with my words. They raced out.

"Go on."

"Okay, you know my family isn't exactly normal. You know about the magic."

He nodded. "I do."

"Well, it seems I had, in fact, gone down with Max to Watchtower Island to do a consultation and stay a few days at Pharaoh's Pointe on Watchtower, owned by the movie producer, Jason Johnson. As it turns out, Jason is part of the Montaigne Lineage. Anyhow, I met Jason's niece Alinka and his two adult daughters, Tessa Johnson and Rita Rocca."

"Okay."

"And while I was down there, I had to protect myself against dark magic generated by Upton Crescent."

"The Magician?" Blake asked.

"You know him."

Panic pangs ignited. Were Blake and Upton...?

Blake shrugged. "Upton's name came up in the police report regarding Alinka's beating."

"So you know about that part?"

"I know what's in the prelim report. There's always stuff that doesn't make it into the report. Upton's name is listed as her boyfriend."

"Okay, well, in the Bahamas, I had to use the Mask of Bluedorf, which is super powerful, to protect myself from Max and Upton, and I fried my powers, and my ancestors whisked me off to Spirit Island over Moon Lake to allow me to heal and wiped my memory which is why I didn't tell Harvey that I knew Alinka. Because they wiped my memory. Are you with me so far?"

Blake kind of half nodded. "I think so. I may need a few moments to sort through this. Go on."

"Okay, so I fainted while I was talking to Harvey, and when I woke up in the ER with Arie standing over me, the doctor said a friend named Max was outside. Arie didn't want to let Max in, but I told Arie it was okay."

Blake's eyebrows raised.

"Look, I knew if I didn't see Max, he'd just keep pestering me. Anyhow, Max said that not only was Alinka beaten, but Tessa and Rita were missing from The Inn outside Plymouth. Arie stayed right outside the door the way Vito's contacts are now."

Blake grabbed his phone, pulled out a stylus, and made a note. "Were they taken in front of Max's eyes? How does he know they are missing?"

"Their phones were left behind, but there was no other trace of them. Arie knows. Max wanted me to talk to Arie with him, but Arie sent a text to Pete, and Pete is following up."

Blake grew quiet for a few minutes. "What aren't you telling me?"

I thought I pretty much told him everything. I was breathless from spewing it all out there. "I think I told you everything."

He took a breath. "Okay, why did Max come to see you? What does he need from you? If you had to use a powerful mask to save yourself rather than rely on Vito's reputation, you had to have been in real danger. What aren't you telling me?"

"You are really good at this cop thing. You know that, right?"

"I do. I seem to remember telling you that more than once when I was doing my best to protect you. You seem to forget that on a regular basis when you go off investigating on your own."

"I will never forget how wonderful you are. I leaned forward and kissed him."

He held me for a moment and then released me. "Nice, but stop trying to distract me. What aren't you telling me?"

"Well, apparently, I am the only one we know who can work the power of the Mask of Bluedorf. And Max believes the Mask and Rita and Tessa are linked."

"Why?"

A vision of me sitting in my home reading Shayla's stolen diary came to mind. And then I flashed to standing in the basement of the house Alex Houston now occupied. The old Caretaker's House. When I grabbed the book that lit up just before Blake's ex shot me.

"The curse mentioned in the diary and the mask are linked. Tessa and Rita are of the 7th generation. I remember when I grabbed that book your ex-was, I saw through the cover something about the coming together of the chosen ones of the 7th generation. I didn't have time to process it because you'd been shot."

"So you think the curse, their disappearance, and the mask are all related?"

"I believe so in my gut."

He looked at me for a minute, but his eye movement indicated he mulled over everything I'd said. "As we discussed, I'm good at being a cop. A magician, not so much. So what have you decided about helping Max?"

"I'm not helping Max, but I have to help Tessa, Rita, and Alinka, as well as their father, and hopefully break the curse."

Blakes scratched the side of his face. "I knew that. I wanted to hear you say it, though. Since magic isn't my specialty, I'm glad Vito is here to guide you."

Voices sounded outside the door.

# CHAPTER 9

I looked through the doors windows. The nurse handed a big white box to one of Vito's contacts. He slid his fingers around the top and inserted his knuckle in the box before pulling it out and knocking on the door.

"Ms. Bracken. This is for you," he said, sitting the box on the bed. The box moved. Blake flinched, and I jumped.

"Don't worry. I checked it," the man I knew only as one of Vito's contacts said.

The lid rocked, and a fluffy black ear popped out, followed by a black and white one. Next, a black button nose and two dark eyes looked at me through a hole before retreating. A black and white giant angora rabbit hopped over Blake's legs and settled into my lap. Fred was back.

I folded over Fred and hugged him. "What's a matter, Fred? Don't trust my human males to protect me?"

His little head wiggled from side to side.

"Man, Bracken, the competition for your heart is tough," Blake said, running his palm along Fred's back. Fred turned to look at Blake as if he was determining who the better male was.

"Don't worry. I've got room in my heart for all of you."

Blake's eyebrows raised for the second time in a few minutes. "All."

"Yes, all, Fred, Sampson, Arie, Vito, and last but certainly not least. What's your name again?" I batted my eyes. "Oh right, Blake. There's room for all of you in my heart."

"Good to know. I was afraid I was going to be replaced. I hate to break up this reunion, but back to the missing women," Blake said.

"Right. Fred showed up in L.A. the day I lost my reflection, and then he appeared on Watchtower Island when Upton blocked my path. Fred helped me channel or control, or whatever the heck it was, I did. So Fred showing up must mean I'm in for another fight. He must be here to help.

"It seems you are getting your memories back," Blake said.

"I think so. I'm just worried about what I'm forgetting."

"If the curse is involved, didn't I remember from one of our early conversations that the Collins Family is related to one of the original families, as is Aire's girlfriend?"

"Yes, Jenna Jasmine is a descendant as wells as the Collins Trio, Arie, and I."

"Again, I need to read up on curses, but I'm good with criminals. If all these people are in jeopardy, we need protection in place. And two variables are in play. What are the conditions of the curses, and what information does the killer have on the curse? Is it your serial killer or a copycat?"

"Sounds like three variables."

"You can count, my lady. I'm impressed."

"Thank you."

"I know the Bracken Lady's Mystery Squad has been working on tracing the descendants. How far along are you? And where is this mask that protects you?"

"Well, that's a long story." I adjusted Fred on my lap. He was trying to eat Blake's blanket.

"How about the condensed version?"

"The Mask was stolen, and the guard who protected it killed. Then when I needed to use it, it appeared in my closet. Now my grandmother's ghosts say it will show up when I need it."

Blake swallowed hard. "So you don't get a chance to practice with it and perfect your powers. It just shows up, and you use it."

I twisted a lock of my hair. Blake had to be thinking, 'run as fast as you can away from this crazy family.' Any sane guy would. But he seemed unphased. And then a thought crossed my mind. What if Blake was a Murker or some other magical coven thing? Maybe that was why he was so calm. Nah, it couldn't be. But then, I would have never guessed Jason Johnson possessed off-screen magic and was related to the Montaignes. It would be just my luck with men that Blake was some kind of super wizard.

"Faith," Blake said.

"Sorry, as far as I know, the mask will just show up when I need it."

Max moved back to his blanket, chewing. "You know I should take Fred home and get him some food and water. I have no idea how long he's been in that box, and I'm sure the hospital staff isn't crazy about him being here."

Blake sent a text to someone. I took the cue to grab a paper cup and tear down the top. After laying Fred on the bed, I walked into the bathroom to fill Fred's water. Blake's phone dinged.

"Vito assures me his contacts are skilled in magical train-ing and special weapons and tactics. So why don't you go home and get Fred situated and grab your notes on the curse? We'll talk later."

"How many times in your life have you put a heroine under the care of a Mob Boss's contacts?"

He smiled. "Don't ask questions; you don't want the answers to."

I gathered up Fred and placed him back in the box, tying the ribbon around it for good measure. I had no doubt Fred could use magic to escape in less than a wink, but the ribbon was for appearances.

As I started to leave the bed, Blake grabbed my hand.

"Faith, my top three detectives on the task force, and I are all in love with women who practice magic. I'm sure there is something philosophical about that, but that's above my pay grade. I want to tell you to walk away from this investigation, but I know you won't, so let us each do what we are good at, and you and the mystery squad handle the magic end. Don't go anywhere without a protection detail. Promise me that."

Tears of love fell down my cheeks. "I promise I won't go anywhere without my protection detail."

"Show me your hands. I want to make sure your fingers weren't crossed." He half-joked, but I knew he meant it.

# CHAPTER 10

Having a protection detail with me at all times was going to be a real pain in the butt. I had no doubt. But, at the same time, I was thankful for the protection. As I left the building with Fred's box in my arm and two of Vito's contacts next to me, Arie, Tiffany, and Vito returned to the hospital. Both men ganged up on me, imploring that I never leave my detail's sights. Arie and Dad made me promise, too. Tiffany sent me silent waves of support.

Luckily, Nothing Fancy had started selling animal feed, bedding, and cages in anticipation of Abracadabra Pet's opening, so they had everything I needed to make Fred comfortable in his new home. I soon learned my protectors were protectors. They didn't carry heavy items because they always required access to their magic weapons and real guns. No one chose to fill me in on the details regarding their magical weapons, and I got the distinct impression that I'd only see the magic weapons when they or I were in grave distress. I crossed my fingers. I'd never see their weapons of any type.

After purchasing everything I needed for Fred at the family discount, Fred, my guys, as I decided to think of them so the whole thing would seem less intense, proceeded to my house. Sampson jumped up and down in front of the windows, barking for all the little guy was worth, although he wasn't so little anymore.

How were Fred and Sampson going to get along? Sampson was used to being the main male in my life, and now I was bringing Fred home and, tomorrow, Blake. I should have grabbed some extra exciting toys for Sampson.

I opened the door, and Sampson burst through and raced for the car, almost as if he knew Fred was inside. One of my guys walked inside and checked my house. I wondered if they had some sort of magic surveillance system. Like I knew my security system checked for human intruders, but was there a system that checked for magic? I needed to find out. Trixie was more forthcoming with magical information than Vito. With Trixie, choice bits of bite-sized magical knowledge and facts spilled from her mouth. Vito, you had to yank info from his mouth.

After unloading the car, it was time to introduce Sampson and Fred. I thought about putting Fred in the cage and letting Sampson sniff him, but I assumed that would make Fred uncomfortable. So I brought Fred inside and placed his box on the couch next to me, and held Sampson on my other side. I untied the bow, and Fred hopped from the box and onto my lap.

Sampson lurched. Fred screamed SIT using a booming voice from my youth that I recognized but couldn't place. Sampson sat, whined, and buried his little nose in my side.

"We need to get a few rules straight," Fred said. "It does no good to lock me in a cage, so don't shut the door. I require a crate for those times when I must meditate in peace; however, I consider a shut door an insult. Two, I will sleep on a pillow on your bed. Sampson may also sleep on the bed, but I will only curl up with him when it is cold. Three, Sampson and I would like a dog door installed. While I can go wherever I need, there may be times when I need backup, and Sampson is not old enough to learn all of my magical tricks. Four, I understand the Jasmine woman is bringing Psychic Cat with her to Abracadabra. I do not like Psychic Cat. He is not allowed in my backyard. We have history."

Well, Okay. I didn't remember Fred being so bossy when we were in the Bahamas. I did save his life in L.A.. And then a scene flashed in my head. Saving Fred started me on the path to home and changed my mind.

"Do you have any other rules?" I asked.

Fred turned his head to look upward and left. "I do, but that's enough for now." He moved next to Sampson and rubbed against him. "We'll be best buds in no time."

Sampson let out a happy bark and jumped off the couch. Fred leaped onto the back of the sofa and then down to the floor. The two zipped to the French doors.

"I take it you two want outside?"

"I'd like to explore my new home and admire the obstacle course Arie built for Sampson. I need to speak to him regarding customizing one for me."

That was one conversation I wanted to witness. "Okay, Fred, you do that. While you two are investigating the backyard, I'll gather my notes in my office." I opened the door and let them outside, and once the door was closed, I raided the goody cabinet for some Double Stuff Oreo Cookies and went inside my office.

Since my encounter with Lisa Bloom and the struggle for the decryption codes, I'd been busy with Trixie's surgery and visiting Blake in the hospital. When Trixie was released from the hospital, I wanted to have the plans for the Magic Factory solidly formed so she could massage the details into place. I hadn't worked much on the curse or the linage.

Tiffany had been tied up with a school project, so she hadn't been able to help. I needed to refresh my memory. The stolen books from my nightstand, which I retrieved from Shayla's hiding place inside the garden center, were now locked away in a safe deposit box right under my nose that I never knew existed. I'd driven by it hundreds of times as a kid, and since I'd been back home. According to Trixie and Vito, only a combination of magic and a unique code could unlock the box. Something told me Vito used the secret place frequently.

I picked up Gerald Lancaster's card. He had told me that several decryption codebooks existed, and they only showed themselves to certain people. So was each book tuned to a specific person or lineage? Like could person A see book A but not book B? Could everyone with the 'gift' see every book? Could some people only see Book A and some people only see book B, but others could see all the books? So many questions. I'd come to believe the books were hidden in Abracadabra, and at least one must be in The Abracadabra Magic Factory. Arie, Blake, and Vito would kill me, but my next stop was the Magic Factory.

I'd been practicing and could now slip into the in-between, leaving my body where it was. I was free to go and do what I wanted and slip back from the in-between. Both Tiff and I had gotten pretty good at it over the last couple of days. My essence could pop over there, and my detail might never know. However, they were magicians too. So I probably should take them with me.

I shoved my notes in my purse, set up Fred's cage and food, and walked to the French doors. Fred sat on the porch munching on a dandelion while Sampson raced through his obstacle course.

"Got to go, guys. Come in for now. I'll stop by the garden center and purchase a dog door. And have Vito or Micky install it ASAP."

Sampson barked once and slid through his last obstacle before dashing inside the door. Fred waited and then followed him inside.

"I'm heading over to the Old Magic Factory before going back to see Trixie. You two be good." I said, closing the door so Fred wouldn't get the last word. I got the feeling the rabbit was an expert in last words.

# CHAPTER 11

"Okay, gentleman," I said to my detail. "We need to make a detour to the Magic Factory before we head back to the hospital. Are you two sure you won't tell me your names? It would make things so much easier."

"You can call me Eagle," said the bigger guy with the bald head. "And call him Stash. He was referring to the shorter, stockier guy with the mustache.

"Eagle and Stash. Thank I've got it."

"With all due respect, Ma'am, I don't think a detour to The Magic Factory is a good idea," Eagle said.

I knew he was going to say that. "What are you two big bad magic warriors afraid of a few ghosts?"

Stash laughed. "No, Ma'am. The magic inside the factory is intense and wonky. We can't guarantee how our powers will respond."

"So, like, will you turn into the Incredible Hulk or something?"

"If we do, we're telling your father it's your fault," Eagle said, turning left toward the factory. "You've been warned."

I mulled over what they meant as I watched a deer run alongside the car. She looked at us as if we were invading her property. While The Bracken Family Trust held the deed and paid the taxes, the animals owned the land from a universal point of view. They maintained it in the natural order. We humans were the ones who took and took from the land. I wanted to change all that. I was anxious to open the Magic Factory, start my seedlings in the ground, and make plans for my first season of The Flower Farm. But I guessed the investigating was the muck I had to walk through first. You'd think with all the horse manure I shoveled on Uncle Cliff's ranch in Montana, I'd have done my time with muck and manure. Guess not.

The car turned into the Magic Factory's drive. Arie must have sent Joey over to work on the back entrance because the potholes and the weeds in the cracks were gone. Wow, Arie must really love Jenna to go to all this work to get the factory in shape. Abracadabra Pets was slated to be one of the first businesses opening in the facility.

The car pulled to a stop in front of the building. Eagle grabbed what looked like a pop can on spindles with little balls attached to the bottom and a micro antenna strapped to the top. Around his wrist, he wore a tiny tablet. "This is a remote-controlled miniature robot with a camera. It will enter first, send back info, and then we'll go inside if all is clear."

"Okay, can that thing pick up magic and dark magic energy as well?"

"We've got something else for that. However, the magical frequencies within the factory distort it, so we have to go old school," Stash said.

"What does old school mean?"

"That's need to know, Ma'am," Eagle said, opening the door to the grand entrance and placing the robot on the floor. "Stay behind us."

I'd walked into the Magic Factory dozens of times by myself, but this was kind of cool in a strange way. I felt like an actor on a police procedural sneaking into the building. But I was here to look for another decryption book, not play private investigator.

"This is a big building, Ma'am. Where do you want to go?"

"Um, I don't really know. I think maybe we should start at the top and work our way down."

Stash's eyes grew wide. "You want to search the whole building? What are we looking for?"

"Well, I'm not quite sure. But I think I'll know it when I see it. We don't have to do the whole thing today. Let's start with the top floor on the south side."

My gut said if the decryption book was here, it was in the secret part of the building that required a descendent to access. Were Stash and Eagle descendants? How did they come to work for Vito? I had so many questions.

But the top floor might be a good choice because it would typically be the last floor searched. Another thought came to me. Were there dummy decryption keys hidden to throw off unscrupulous searches who might have just enough talent to find them—say, a family's black sheep?

Was the book Lisa forced me to find and then she stole real or fake? The elders or originals, or whatever the founding Abracadabra Colonists called themselves, went to massive lengths to guarantee their work wouldn't fall into the wrong hands. Thus, fake spells and decryption books were a definite probability. And what happened when a fake fell into evil hands? Did it just not work, or did it attack the evildoer? So many questions?

I took a few more steps forward, following my detail. A flash of Blake and Shayla getting it on in the room on the first floor came to me. What if Shalya knew about the decryption codes, and she brought Blake and whoever else here to unwittingly protect her while she scanned for the books? If I could see them, could Shayla? I needed to ask Blake how many rooms they'd used. That was going to be an interesting conversation.

"You know what, guys? I need more info before we start searching to develop a better plan." That sounded like lingo that would resonate with their training.

"Okay, Ma'am, if that's what you'd like to do," Eagle said.

"What I'd like is for you to stop calling me Ma'am or Ms. Bracken. It makes me sound old. Call me Faith, please. Tell Vito I insist."

"Okay." As we followed the pop can on wheels robot toward the front entrance, a knocking noise came from the southwest hallway, which led to the storage barns. Thinking of Tessa and Rita, I turned and sprinted down the hall.

A large hand grabbed my arm. "Faith, wait. Let us send the robot."

"But it could be Tessa and Rita."

"And the killer could be there. You can't help them if you are dead."

He had a point. "Okay, well, then get the robot in gear."

"I can tell you are Trixie's daughter," Stash said.

I got the feeling that wasn't meant as a compliment. But I decided to take it that way. The robot thing rolled down the hallway ahead of us. When it was halfway to the knocking, Eagle released my arm, and we crept toward the sound.

If there were someone or something inside the door bent on hurting us, wouldn't my magic signal me? I had to believe it would. The rhythm increased. Two more lovers, perhaps? Shayla was in jail, and Blake was in the hospital.

The robot stopped at the door. A scream blasted my eardrums. The noise came from inside the room. I knew that scream. Stash and Eagle drew their guns and crouched low.

"You can put down your weapons, guys. I've got this. I opened the door and found a red fox family playing inside. Someone had opened a window, and these furry critters had taken it as an invitation."

I stood in the doorway. A part of me wanted to kick them out, but they obviously needed a home. "Okay, listen, dudes. I know you need a home. You can stay one more night while I set up a home for you in the morning, but tomorrow you're being relocated."

I closed the door and reopened it as something flashed on my mental screen. The wall behind an ancient copy machine glowed purple. I stepped inside the room. Eagle grabbed my hand.

"I don't think it's a good idea. Those things could have rabies."

"You grew up in the city, didn't you, Eagle?"

"Guilty."

"I got this, Eagle. I promise. I may need a pocketknife, though. Does either of you have one?"

"You aren't planning to stab one, are you?" Stash asked.

I wanted to laugh but thought better of it. They were, after all, willing to die to save me.

"Nope, I promise. I will not stab the foxes or you two. I need to open the wall."

Stash tossed me his knife.

"Thanks." Staying close to the wall, I allowed the foxes their space and an exit point through the opened window should they feel the need to retreat while I made my way to what had once served as a copier. I vaguely remembered watching Grams use one like it in the garden center office when I was five or six.

When I arrived at the glowing spot, I placed my hand on it. It was warm but not like a fire. Running my hand up and down the wallboard, I found a place above and below that was cool to my touch. I stuck the knife in both areas. A little door swung open. Stash and Eagle raised their guns.

# CHAPTER 12

Inside the opened door was a black wooden container with brass plates and hinges about the size of a child's jewelry box. "Open With Care!" was engraved on the plate under the latch.

I looked at Stash and Eagle. "You guys obviously know more about this magic stuff than I do. It says open with care. Should I wait until we get outside?"

"Well, it presented to you and not us," Stash said. "Listen to the magic. What is it telling you to do?" I placed the box on the old desk and pushed the little locking mechanism. It clicked, and the lid sprung open. A part of me expected to see a genie or Aladdin pop out. Instead, a swirl of brightly colored magic dust spiraled upward toward the ceiling and filtered around the room before most of it drifted out the door, and some went out the window.

"That is magic dust, right?" I asked.

"Um, yes," Eagle said. "It appears to be. I've never seen it behave like that. Usually, you throw dust or summon your dust. It doesn't travel by itself."

"Unless someone with supreme magic juice summoned it," I said. That thought scared my socks off. Something was at the bottom of the box, but I couldn't get to it because of the dust's velocity.

"When a person calls their dust, it comes to them. It doesn't trail. It would take a supreme entity to cause the dust to swirl, and they would have led you to it, knowing you had the power to unleash it," Stash said.

Two things came to mind. Upton Crescent and The Mask of Bluedorf. Both were frightening possibilities. Where was that darn Lighter when I had questions? It had been MIA for a couple of days now.

"There's still something on the bottom. I can't get to it because of all the dust flying in my face."

Stash entered the room, walked to the windows, and opened a second one, careful not to block the foxes' exit point. He stuck his hand out the window and snapped his fingers twice. A gas mask appeared in his hands. Cool!

Wow, I wanted to learn that trick.

After placing the mask on his head, he inched along the wall to the table and peered into the box before reaching inside and withdrawing a brass key about four inches long and as thick as a deadbolt. There was also a little memo book under the key.

He handed the book to me and took off his gas mask. "What does it say?"

"I don't know. I don't see any words on the page." I flipped from page to page. Stash crowded over my shoulder.

"There is a message. It's just not for you," said the voice I'd come to know as The Lighter.

Think of the devil.

"I assure you; I am not the devil."

A swarm of dragonflies and butterflies danced around outside the window. Usually, the Lighter presented as one or the other. Maybe the dust had made it stronger.

"So whose eyes is this display for?" I asked. "And why did you show it to me if it wasn't for me?"

"Keep it with you. You'll know who can read it."

I closed the lid on the box and tucked it under my arm. The box struggled under my hold. "Would it kill you to give me a straight answer? Is it against some kind of Lighter code?"

"Why don't you ask me about the dust?"

A commotion in the corner caught my attention. The foxes stood upright on their back legs, jumped into the air, and touched their noses to the ceiling. Then they dropped back to the floor, rolled over, and shook their little butts. And did it all over again. Their energy had changed from frightened when we first walked in to elated. These critters were having the time of their lives.

"What's in that dust?" Eagle asked.

One of the baby foxes jumped in my arms and licked my face before hopping back down and rolling over three times.

"You'll see and figure it out. When you do, more keys will be revealed. However, before you can fully ignite all the powers, you must capture the one killing our people."

"If you have access to the power, why aren't you?"

"Because I must work at a higher level. The curse and the killer are the seventh generation's responsibility."

"Of course. Why would it be any different? Okay. Keys. Real metal keys? Keys that unlock things?" I asked.

"Everything is real, and nothing is real. All keys unlock."

I'd had it with all the mumbo jumbo. "Lighter, I think you make things up as you go along. I don't think you know what you are talking about."

Stash and Eagle backed up.

A peacock feather appeared in the space beside my face, and it caressed my skin. "Ah, Faith. You are so like your mother." A whoosh followed its words, and it was gone.

"Ms. Bracken," Stash said. "You've got guts. No one talks to the Lighter as you did, except Trixie."

I took the box and marched from the room. Okay, so I was more like my family than I cared to admit. I guess you could take the woman away from the Brackens, but not the Brackens out of the woman.

When we were outside the magic factory, I put a rock on the top of the lid to reinforce the lock. It was probably better not to release any more dust until we understood what it did.

As we exited the grand entrance, Stash stopped. "Do you feel that?"

I halted behind him. "I don't feel it as much as see it."

"I hear it," Eagle said. "The air is alive. It's snapping, popping, and crackling, like my cereal, only it's everywhere."

He was right. For me, hundreds of thousands of fairy-sized particles formed into waves and then shot past and through me at lightning speed. What had I just done?

# CHAPTER 13

W hen I brought the box home, Fred planted his black and white Angora butt on its lid and refused to leave. Sampson climbed on top of the coffee table next to Fred and placed his puppy nose on the container as well. When I yelled at Sampson to get down, Fred scolded me that they were performing important work and ordered me to leave them alone. Wonder if there's an obedience school for magical talking rabbits.

I'd been up to see Trixie, but she was still pretty out of it, and the nurses said she'd be that way until tomorrow. I popped in to see Blake, but he was also asleep. Growing up, I'd always known Vito's contacts were around because he told us they'd report back to him if we were bad. Arie never cared. I did. So while we knew they were there, I never noticed the contacts, which is why they were good at their jobs. After spending every last minute with Stash and Eagle since the bones appeared, I determined Vito had a whole army under his command. Two were outside Trixie's room, and two were outside Blake's. Interesting.

I'd gotten word from Arie. Tiffany, Vito, and he were coming over and spending the night to protect me, and we would be dining in. He ordered me to "get cracken on the cookin."

Instead, I ordered a few twenty-inch pizzas, breadsticks, and salads from the pizza place in Moon Lake. Kat, the owner, delivered them as my family arrived.

"I thought you were cooking," Vito said.

"Your message didn't stipulate I had to cook. Plus, I didn't have time. There have been developments we need to discuss. So dig in."

Tiff flipped open a lid. "I'm starving. And I can always eat pizza."

I agreed. My stomach had been rumbling for hours, but I was too overwhelmed by the super-duper magic dust to eat. Now my hunger roared.

"So tell us about these developments," Vito said before sticking half a slice in his mouth at one time.

"Not until my tummy is full. I need to experience the pleasure of these flavors."

"I just devour," Arie said. He put his pizza down long enough to open the door and invite Stash and Eagle inside and two more men I didn't know existed. They came inside one by one, grabbed a slice or two, and exited, doing their bests to be invisible.

I'd been joking about experiencing the pleasure of the flavors, but wow. This was the best pizza ever. Like really ever. I'd never had pizza this amazing. The flavors were deep and rich and exploded in my mouth. And I'd bet I knew why.

"What did you have them do to this pizza?" Tiffany asked. "Moon Lake Pizza is always good, but tonight it's incredible."

"I was thinking the same thing," Arie said.

Vito looked at me. "You found it, didn't you?" A frown and narrowed eyes contorted his face a bit.

"My guard animals have it under animal pay and nose." I motioned to the coffee table.

"Let me guess. That's the development," Vito grumbled.

Arie's attention focused on us.

"Just tell us," Tiff said before dipping her breadstick into the cheese sauce.

"She found a stash of the mythical Alchemist's Dust," Vito said.

Arie studied Vito's trouble reaction. "How is it different from the magic dust we carry? I don't have Faith's superior body language reading skills, but I'm a cop. You aren't pleased she found it. When I took your brand new caddy for a joyride at age eight, you made that same face.

Vito pushed away from the breakfast bar and walked over to the box. "These are supposed to contain a warning." He knelt to examine the outside.

"It said open with care. I was careful."

"But you didn't think maybe you should consult with me first."

I shrugged. "I considered it, and then my intuition told me to open it."

"So you did," Tiffany smirked. "Stop stalling, Grandpa, and tell us about the dust. How is it different?"

Vito sighed. "Okay, let's clean up, and I'll tell you what I remember. I've never seen the dust work. We've known deposits of it existed."

Dinner disappeared, and a few minutes later, we were gathered around the coffee table. Vito opened the door and whistled. Six of his contacts strode through the door. "I want you all to see this and hear the story."

Vito took his place in front of the box. "Fred, Ole Fellow, I need you to release your position. They should see this work. You and Sampson too."

"I don't think opening the box just yet is a good idea. We are not prepared."

"I get that, Fred, but they must see it in action so I can prepare them."

Fred thumped his back feet and hopped off the box. "Well, give Sampson and me a chance to get close to the screen door before you open it. That dust is nasty in our lungs. Follow me, Sampson."

Vito twirled his fingers and snapped them twice. He pushed the lever, and a rainbow of magic dust rose & spiraled from inside, filling the room in seconds.

"Wow," Tiffany said. "It's amazing. I can't take my eyes off of it."

A car pulled into the driveway. Car doors shut. Arie went to the window. Vito reached to close the lid.

"No, Dad, leave it open. Pete and Link are here. They need to see this." Arie opened the door and let them in.

"What the heck?" Pete said. "I've heard the legend, but never seen it. Howard Crane was going on about it in Grace's bookstore the other day. He was terrified someone would return."

The dust continued to rise and swirl. Some of it escaped out the screen door when the two detectives arrived.

Vito shut the lid. "Now, close your eyes for a moment. I'll tell you when to open them."

I did as I was told. From the silence, I believed the others did as well. "Open your eyes," Vito said roughly thirty seconds later. "What do you see?"

"The air is alive," Pete said. "I've never seen anything like this in all my time with Monique. It shimmers."

"And tinkles," Tiffany said. "Like hundreds of thousands of little bells. I smell Vanilla."

Arie ran his hands up and down his arms. "It tingles."

"Link, Pete, do you have time to hear the legend? Or do you need Arie stat?" Vito asked.

"I've been around Monique long enough to believe whatever is in this legend might help us solve our cases. Enlighten us, Vito," Pete said, grabbing a barstool.

Tiffany walked into the kitchen. "Talk slow, Grandpa. I need popcorn. I'm making a triple batch."

Arie sent her an evil stare. Tiff ignored him.

"Long ago, no one knows exactly when. A group of alchemists from the North, South, East, and West were led to Abracadabra by a powerful being. Some versions of the legend say the being was alien. Others believed Universal Power beckoned the first alchemists. The number was rumored to be four, but most of us think that number was much more significant—a small colony. And we believe those who came were a mixture of alchemists, witches, magicians, witch doctors, psychics, and spiritualists.

"The legend says once the colonists were here, incredible powers were bestowed upon them with the trust that they would carry those powers and create a magical world. But they were soon attacked regularly by evil forces who wanted to control others through fear and manipulation, and there were riffs within the colony. Some were expelled.

"Fearing their work would be stolen and used for evil, legend says several caches of Alchemist Dust and other items were hidden and tuned so that only specific lineages could find the dust when the time warranted it. I believe

Abracadabra and Moon and Echo Lakes are calling their descendants home to work the magic. Based on reports out of The Allegro Islands, we believe the islands are also somehow connected and calling her lineage home."

"OMG, Turk," came out of my mouth.

"Yes," said Vito. "Although we aren't as sure what's happening on Allegro."

"Turk, your old college boyfriend?" Arie asked. "For the record, I liked him."

"Me too," said Vito.

I rolled my eyes in response.

"So what does this dust do?" Tiff asked again.

"It magnifies and enhances everything and is stronger than any prescription or street drug."

"How?" Tiff asked.

"Just as the pizza's flavors were exponentially better and the wave particles are now visible. Look at the couch. If you stare at the couch for a moment, you'll see the molecules moving."

I focused for a second. Dad was right. I couldn't actually see the molecules, but I did see the couch in waves.

"So what is it good for other than a high?" Tiff asked.

"It magnifies everything, which means if you surround yourself with the dust, it magnifies everything you are. If you think about riding an elephant for more than five seconds, an elephant will appear. If you think about a Lamborghini, one will appear in the driveway, but if you think dark thoughts, those happen as well. If you were to curse someone, it would immediately happen. Most important. You have to live with the consequences of your thoughts. If you think of a cow, you have to shovel its dung. Come with me to the window."

We gathered around. "Look at the old dead tree out in the middle of the field. I've been meaning to cut it down since I arrived. What do you see?"

"It's not dead," Pete said. "It's alive with activity."

"You get an A, Pete. Now, I want you all to think about the tree lying on the ground in a dead tree position. Kill the tree."

"I can't," I said.

Vito rolled his eyes. "Just humor me."

I closed my eyes and visualized the tree lying on the ground, dead.

"Wow," said Tiffany. "It's down. But I didn't see or hear it fall."

"Here's the cool part. Stand it back up. See it thriving. And instead of viewing it as dead. See it as vibrant as some of the trees we have for sale."

That I could do. I closed my eyes and pictured the tree as it was in my youth. Strong and tall and brave.

"Open your eyes," Vito said.

I cried. The tree that I had climbed, fallen from, and wept under was back in all her glory.

"When the Alchemist's Dust is present, you have to police your thoughts as if they were nuclear because they are."

"Which is why I think opening the box was a mistake," Fred said. "Humans can't police their thoughts twenty-four seven. It's not in their nature."

"So cop here," Arie said. "What kind of range does this dust have, and how long does it last?"

"That is the unknown."

Fred hopped back over and sat on the lid. "You know, I can't sit on this forever. We need to put it somewhere safe."

"I agree with the rabbit," Link said. "If this stuff fell into the wrong hands. Does it have a fail-safe?"

"My name is Fred. While I present as a rabbit, I am many things. The Alchemist Dust is only the tip of the iceberg. An iceberg. We need to melt if we are to save Tessa and Rita."

"Can we use the dust to find them?" Tiffany asked.

"I don't know," said Vito. "I do know certain caches are tuned to certain lineages and specific people within those lineages."

"How could the elders tune for people who weren't born yet?" I asked.

"Ah, that magic is above even my pay grade."

"So you are saying the Alchemists knew I or Aire or Monique would be here at this time, and they knew what our frequencies would be?"

"It appears to be the case," Fred answered for Vito.

Tiffany hugged herself. "I just had a chill run up and down my spine."

I experienced the same feeling. "So back to the original curse, we began by tracing four families. The Brackens, The Montaignes, The Collins, and The Jasmines, but from what you are saying, there could be other lineages we aren't aware exist."

Vito nodded. "My guess would be at least one or two of them have to be of Native American descent. They occupied this land at the time The Alchemist arrived. It would make sense at least a family or two integrated into the colony."

"And if I understand right. The Murkers were kicked out. Which means there are probably others who were expelled as well."

"That is correct," said Fred. "However, The Murkers are our most powerful enemy. We need to defeat them first."

"The Lighter said first we need to stop the person who is killing our people. So is the serial killer a Murker?"

Fred wiggled on the box. "We don't have evidence to make a definite conclusion."

"Okay, Bailey, Blake's ex-sister-in-law, was part of my generation, as were Rhonda Prescott, Calvin, Sheryl, and Anita. They were all descendants but died at the hands of different people, in different places, at different times. So is the curse using others to kill them? Is the curse killing them? Or is the curse getting them to put themselves in positions where they'll be killed?

I sat in my chair and let the questions I'd ask roll over me. Once we wrapped up the curse, I thought we'd be done and could move on. But wow. My mind reeled.

"So that's why opening The Magic Factory is so critical. We must teach our people the ways of magic to defeat the darkness. I heard my mouth say."

"Grandpa, who do you work for? I know you're supposed to be a mob boss and all, but I believe that's a cover. Who do you really work for?"

Vito smiled. "It's better if you don't know."

"That's not an answer."

"This is a lot to process," Link said, changing the subject. "Grace's bookstore received a large anonymous delivery of old books related to local legends and magic. The books randomly appeared on the dock. It took Syd and me two hours to carry them inside and put them in the workroom. Howard Crane begged Grace to burn them all. That shipment might contain more answers. Or it could produce more questions. Right now, we've got three missing women to find and a beating to solve. I understand we are handling the police part while you all handle the magic part."

"That's right," Arie said, standing. "You needed me. Three missing women?"

Link nodded. "We learned Amy Prescott, Rhonda Prescott's younger sister, was reported missing by her employers in Muncie. She works for the university and lives a few miles from campus. She's been gone a couple of days. We need all hands on deck. I know the Prescotts tie into the original family legend. Fingers have already started to point toward Alex Houston."

"And with the magic dust loose and those who believe Alex is still guilty," Vito said before sending a text and looking at his contacts. "Stash, Eagle, go pick up Alex Houston and take him to a safe house. With Amy in Muncie, I don't understand how people can think Alex is responsible. It's crazy, but crazy people do crazy things."

# CHAPTER 14

After the unveiling of The Alchemist's Dust Myth, Arie left with Pete and Link. Vito scooped up the box with the dust, and he and Fred disappeared too.

"What if we need that dust to protect ourselves?" I had asked.

"Don't worry," Fred said. "Now that you've interacted with the dust, it will come when you call it."

"And how do I call it? Here, Dust. Here, Dust."

Fred thumbed his back legs in response. The rabbit needed to lighten up a bit. "Just ask for it to assist you." He hopped out the door trailing Vito.

This morning, both Vito, Arie, and Fred were still out and about. I'd just started a pot of coffee for our detail outside when Tiffany came downstairs dressed in black jeans and a black T-shirt with a giant rose on it. "I decided I needed to start branding my appearance. What do you think? Does the shirt say Flower Witch?"

I looked more closely and saw a broomstick coming out of the center of the rose. "Wow, that's fantastic. Where'd you get it?"

"I printed it on this printer we have at school." I placed a plate filled with bacon, eggs, and sausage in front of her. "Are you thinking what I am?" she asked.

"Well, I think I need to make a trip to Grace's Rare Books today. I talked to Blake already. They aren't releasing him until this evening. They want to run one more test. He, being a guy, didn't seem to know what the test was. Was a trip to Grace's on your mind?"

"Yep," Tiff said before stuffing a forkful of eggs into her mouth.

An hour later, Tiffany and I entered Grace's Rare Book in Moon Lake. Grace hugged us both and led us toward the back.

"Link sent me a text last night and filled me in. I've started pulling some things that might be of help. I'm trying to be on the sly about this, or Howard will go ballistic again."

"What's his deal?" Tiffany asked.

Grace shrugged. "Howard is Howard. That's my only explanation."

Grace's assessment of Howard Crane was spot on. He was who he was. Quirks, grips, growls, and wild conclusions. And yet, he was Moon Lake's beloved fixture.

"Link said these books just appeared out of nowhere," I prodded.

Grace opened the door to her workroom. The smell of old books mixed with the energy of wonder and magic. I'd been in here as a kid, playing with Grace's daughter, Sydney Hoven. I'd never seen it so full. Un-opened boxes sat from floor to ceiling, and books were spread across two long tables.

Grace sat down and rubbed her forehead. "Last Wednesday, when I opened the door, they were sitting on the dock. There were enough to fill half a semi-trailer. All of what I've opened so far relate to myth and magic or the area's history. As you can see, I haven't opened even half of the boxes."

Grace's attention went to Stash, who entered the room.

"Stash and Eagle are with us. Arie, Blake, and Vito decided we needed protection."

"I heard. Link and Pete have Sydney, Monique, and Elle locked down in a secret hiding place. Should you need to escape for any reason, exit that door right there. You'll figure it out and be safe."

"Thank you."

"No problem. I will feel much better when this curse thing is put to bed. Since I heard some of the details, I feel the need to keep Syd, Monique, and Elle on a short leash. I know they are grown women, but you are all Tiffany's age to me. Uncle Bob trained us to shoot, but he didn't school us in magic."

Monique had explored her magical gifts as a teenager. She was teased unmercifully in high school. Arie being one of the worst perpetrators.

"That's a lot of books to go through," Tiffany said, interrupting my memories. "We'll be here until Christmas."

I had to agree with her. The task was daunting. And then an image flashed in my mind. "Maybe not."

"What?" Tiff asked, carrying the first box to the table.

"The book on the wall before Blake was shot lit up when I was close. And The Alchemists Dust lit up as well. So..."

Howard Crane banged on the window. "Did you just say, The Alchemist's Dust?" He ran as fast as his sandals, seventies guru pants, and old legs would allow him around the corner. As he neared the workroom, our detail blocked his path.

"Faith, get these goons out of my path this minute."

"It's okay, Eagle. Let Howard through. We go way back."

Howard plopped down into a chair opposite Tiff. He eyed her for a moment and must have decided she was okay.

"Did I hear correctly? Did you find The Alchemists Dust? Oh no, it has started. I didn't think it would happen this soon. The missing women. The Dust. I warned you, tromping in the past is never a good idea. You opened it and let some go. That's why I've been so off the last twenty-four. This is bad. This is really bad."

"Mr. Crane, why don't you calm down and tell us what's started," Tiffany said.

His head shook. He had trouble getting up from his chair. "Wait, wait, I must go get my notes. Goons, I am glad you are here. I hope you are carrying my latest invention. The M191. You will need it soon." Howard ran at top Howard speed toward the far corner of the store.

Grace stuck her head in. "What happened?"

"He heard me say something about the Alchemists' Dust and bolted."

"Mr. Crane mumbled, 'it's started.' He had to go get his notes," Tiff added.

"Well, he ran out the front door and left his stuff here. So he must have gone home. He's never done that. Ever. Whatever he knows must be pretty important."

"How wacko is he?" Tiffany asked.

Grace smiled and sat down. "Howard is eccentric and opinionated, but Howard has a crazy high I.Q. and a good heart. He's been a staple in this bookstore since the day I opened. And while he'd kill me for saying this, Howard has arranged for gifts to be delivered to many a household who needed a helping hand, all of it anonymous. He's never told me, but I figured it out after people had shared their stories with me, Melba, or the librarian, and the next day, a gift came. Howard has always been the common denominator in the room."

"How did he make his money?" I asked. "I didn't remember Howard working a day in his life."

"Part of it was family money, but most of it was good investing, and Howard owns patents on numerous inventions."

"So he's a genius, rich, wacko," Tiffany said. I kicked her under the table.

Grace burst into laughter. "True. His family has been in the area forever. His linage has to be wrapped up in all of this. He doesn't have any children I know of, so he wouldn't have a daughter in danger. I don't know why he is all worked up."

"Well, if he comes back, I guess we'll find out. I think I have an idea. According to The Lighter, if what we are searching for is here, we'll know it. When I found the decryption key, it lit up, as did the Magic Dust. Going on that theory, maybe if we run our hands over the boxes, the boxes will light up."

"Sounds like a plan," Grace said.

"Wait," said Stash. "The Lighter said, 'if it was meant for you.' I took that to mean there could be other items meant for someone else that wouldn't light up for you."

I slumped in my chair. He was right. "You know you just killed my bright idea, right?"

"Maybe not totally." Stash continued. "Perhaps you each need to run your hands over the boxes. What works for one of you may not work for the other. Ms. Hovan, I would suggest getting your daughter and her cousins in her as well, since you all are part of the founding families."

"Good thinking, Stash," I said. So Stash and Eagle were more than just muscle. Good to know. "Thank You. Too bad Link and Pete have them sequestered away."

"Give me five minutes, and I can have them here for you." Grace walked through the door she'd indicated as a safe exit. I assumed that the door led to the old theatre. Maybe the guys had them holed up in there.

"Okay, Tiff, with all those boxes, we'd better get craken." I started on one end and Tiffany on the other.

"What do I do?" Tiff asked.

"I plan to put my hand on the box and count to five. If I sense something, I'll set the box to the side to go through."

"Sounds good."

We both finished the first row vertically. Tiffany had set one box to the side. Eagle placed it on the table. I must have looked at him funny.

"Both Stash and I have ties to the original families and sisters. It looks like helping you solve this case and ending the curse saves our jobs and families. Before you ask, our sisters have been moved to secure locations."

So how big was my father's operation? Someday he was going to tell us if I had to beat it out of him.

"It must be tough for you here, guarding us while your sisters could be at risk."

"Part of the job," Stash said.

"I've got something," Tiffany said. She was correct. The box at the very top glowed a rich ruby color. Eagle stepped in and grabbed the container.

I was on my third stack when my hand started tingling, and the third box from the top turned a bright pumpkin orange. Stash held the other two up while I pulled the pumpkin-colored box out. Eagle placed it on the table.

As we both neared the center, we found three more boxes. "Well, that was easier than I thought," Tiffany said. "Now, if the info we need is highlighted and decoded, we'd be in great shape."

"We can hope." Magic was never that simple.

We were about to sit down and start opening the boxes when Grace walked through the safe door, followed by Monique, Elle, and Sydney. And Howard came through the other door.

"I knew it. I knew you'd gather the troops," Howard said. "This is bad. Really bad. He's coming. He's coming."

"Mr. Crane, I think you need to sit down," Tiffany said. Grace pulled a chair close to Howard. Sydney moved to help lower him into the chair.

The room heaved and bellowed a deep belly sort of laugh. Howard screamed. He was gone.

Stash grabbed my arm. "Ladies, get back to your safe room." Eagle's hand wrapped around Tiff's waist. "We need to get to the car. Ladies, now. Get to your safe room." They ushered us from the room. Tiffany grabbed a box on her way out, and I did as well.

"We'll return these soon," I yelled to Grace.

"I'm not worried," Grace replied. I looked over my shoulder and around Stash to see Grace put the closed sign on the door.

# CHAPTER 15

S econds later, Tiff and I were in a black SUV speeding out of Moon Lake toward Abracadabra.

"Who laughed?" Tiffany asked. "Where is Mr. Crane? Will he be all right? And who is the he, Mr. Crane said, was here?"

"And is the he who was there, the serial killer?" I asked.

Stash turned in his seat. "Ma'am, this is my assessment. Powerful dark energy entered the room at the speed of a laser. The energy laughed at us."

"Wow, that's super helpful, Stash," Tiff said.

"I state the facts."

Tiffany leaned forward to look Stash in the eyes while Eagle drove. "What will happen to Mr. Crane? Did it take him, or did he disappear to save himself?"

"I don't know," Stash said. "Mr. Crane is a legend in the Lighter's Community. Both scenarios are possible. The best thing we can do is get you two home."

The speed limit on this road was fifty. Our SUV had to be doing ninety. Trees blurred by.

"Are we safe at home? If it got to us in the bookstore. It can get to us anywhere, can't it? When you say you have your sisters in a secure location, how can you know that? How can Grace, Pete, and Link know that the Collins

Trio is safe? If the dark energy could get to them in the bookstore, how can they be safe anywhere?" I asked. "I think I like human villains better. At least you can lock your doors."

I swore Eagle took that corner on two wheels. Tiffany and I both swayed left and were forced to hold on. A cold chill radiated in my spin. Tiff grabbed my hand. She felt it too. A vision flashed for less than a nanosecond in my mind.

"In-Between," Tiff and I yelled at the same time. I grabbed Stash with my right hand. Tiff snatched Eagle's arm. Together we dove into the In-Between and pulled our bodies out of the car and into a deep ravine on the side of the road. Eagle's legs got caught in the seat belt. Stash dove back through and yanked on Stash's leg. I held my breath. Tiff squeezed my hand. Imagine the loudest thunder you've ever heard, magnified by one thousand. The ground shook so hard, two trees toppled.

"Eagle," I screamed.

"Stash, Stash, where are you?" Tiffany cried.

The tree above us rattled. I looked up. Both men climbed down as Tiffany and I crawled up the ravine and onto the side of the road.

The cows in the pasture across the street gathered in the corner farthest away from us. Old Mr. Willis, in his denim blue Studebaker, pulled to a stop.

"Everyone okay?" He opened his truck door and extended a hand to Tiff and me as we tried to stand. My legs shook, but I managed to stay upright. Tiffany wrapped her arms around me. Mr. Willis kept his hand on my back. Sirens sounded in the distance.

Someone must have heard the explosion and called in an emergency. The SUV was reduced to puzzle piece size. All the king's horses and all the king's men couldn't put the SUV back together. It wasn't happening. Most of the vehicle was now dust. A second later, the four of us would have returned to ashes.

"How in tarnation did you survive?" Mr. Willis asked.

"I don't really know," I answered.

The sirens were now so loud I couldn't hear myself think. Brakes squealed. Had to be Arie. Slamming on the brakes was the only way he knew to stop a car. His door slammed, followed by several others.

"What the heck happened?" He asked, hugging both Tiffany and me.

"You're a detective, Dad. Do we have to explain it to you?" Tiff asked.

"That's not what I mean, and you know it, smart butt."

"We were at Grace's bookstore this morning, looking through boxes of old books chasing a lead. Howard Crane heard me mention The Alchemist's Dust. Monique, Sydney, and Elle came into the workroom to help us look. Then Howard came in, and dark energy laughed. Howard disappeared, and Stash and Eagle dragged us to the car. Seconds before the car exploded, both Tiff and I received a warning, and we slipped into the In-Between and got out before it was blown to smithereens," I said.

"Sir, I believe we need to get them home immediately," Stash said to Aire. "The dark energy was powerful, possibly magnified by the dust."

"Where can they go where the darkness can't touch them? How am I supposed to fight a villain I can't see?" Arie yanked his hand through his hair.

"Sir," Eagle said, "They will be safe inside Faith's house?"

Arie spread his legs and crossed his arms, rocking slightly forward to his toes. "How do you know that?"

"Because we've fortified the house since the prior incidents. Dark energy cannot penetrate Faith's house, your house, or Vito's."

"I assume my father ordered this."

"He did, and before you ask, I am not at liberty to tell you how we did it. Just know that it is done. I also believe you should come with us."

Arie raked his hands through his thick hair again and walked in a circle, kicking pebbles from his path. He really was going to be bald if he continued. I needed to buy him a hair net.

A man with a TV Camera yelled Arie's name.

"Arie, what happened? Can we get a statement?"

"The only statement I am making is to get back. We need room to work."

"Faith, my dear, are you all right?" A familiar voice said from the other side of a police car.

Howard was correct. He was here. Upton Crescent stood in front of a television camera, and Max was with him.

"Faith and I are old friends," he said to the camera. "She used to work for my brother's company."

I couldn't help myself.

# CHAPTER 16

Nor did I care a television crew was filming. In hindsight, I wanted them to be there. I needed the world to know what a horrible scumbag Upton Crescent was. And I'm not sure how I got from beside Arie and Stash to Upton so fast. Anger is powerful.

"Upton, you did this. You tried to kill us. What the heck is the matter with you? Max, what are you doing with him? You two abducted Tessa and Rita the way you tried to get to me on Watchtower Island. Well, guess what? You aren't going to win. I will not let you hurt anyone else in your quest for ultimate power. And you, Max, do not, and I repeat this so your stupid brain can figure it out. Max, do not come near me again, or I will have you arrested."

Upton reached for my hand. I pulled it away. "Do not touch me."

The power surging through me was incredible. Like power I'd never experienced before. "Max, you are a toad for coming to me and then hanging with Upton. I'm out of here." The crowd gasped.

My left sneaker stood behind my kitchen island.

I was entirely inside my house. OMG. Had I just turned Max into a toad and disappeared in front of a news reporter?

I dropped onto my pink couch and buried my head in my hands on my knees. What had I done? How did I fix this? See, this is why they warn you off of magic because it's so complex and a strict code to live by. Vito, Trixie, and Arie were going to kill me. And for what? What did we achieve today? We got Howard captured and our SUV blown to pieces along with the books we'd found.

Did I have to stay on magic's path? There had to be some way to refuse it and move on with a nice everyday life. Had to be.

Sampson ran to the office door and pawed at the door. That was Sampson's speech for "let me out." Why he couldn't use the French doors two feet from me, I didn't understand, but getting up and caring for him was better than wallowing in my pity.

Wiping my face and drying my tears on the hem of my red boyfriend shirt, I walked into my office and fell nose-first over something. Sampson licked my right cheek while my left cheek kissed the rug. My pup thought we were playing a game and jumped over me like I was one of the obstacles in his course. Putting my arms up to shield my face from Sampson's enthusiasm, I looked back at the door. Six boxes of books, just like the ones we'd left on Grace's worktable and the ones Tiff and I had grabbed on the way out, were strewn around my office.

Tiff's foot and part of her leg landed a foot from my head. The rest of her came through, and she opened the door to let Sampson outside.

"Sorry, when I sent the boxes here, I should have done a better job stacking them. I'll put that on my practice sheet."

"How?"

"I've been practicing. Depending on the situation, I place or pull objects into the In-Between and send them wherever I want. When I'm in class, I send my backpack from class to class. It gives me more time to grab a snack between classes. I'm almost as good as some of the big named delivery services. I'm thinking of starting my own company." She reached down and offered me a hand up.

"When we exited Grace's, I sent the boxes we'd separated from the stacks, and when we jumped from the car, I sent the other boxes. I assumed there must be something in these the darkness didn't want us to find."

I shoved the offending box out of my way and walked to the kitchen to retrieve some ice for my cheek. "I know another father raised you, but you've got a lot of Arie in you, girlfriend."

Tiffany laughed. "I know. And while I miss the father who raised me for the first part of my life, I'm lucky to have the opportunity to live as Arie's daughter. Trust me; my life was never as exciting as it is now."

Brakes squealed outside. "I wonder how many sets of brakes your father goes through in a year?"

"He could put me through college on what he spends on brake jobs."

# CHAPTER 17

Footsteps sounded outside the door. "I'm Law Enforcement. I need to speak with Faith." Outstanding, the day wasn't even half over, and already I'd listened to Howard rant and disappear, encountered and run from darkness, jumped in the nick of time from an exploding car, looked like a crazed freak on television, and now one of the two princes of darkness was on my front porch.

I went to the door and opened it. "Harvey, I thought my father said if you had more questions for me to go through my lawyer."

"You realize your disappearing act today puts your alibi for all the murders in question. Don't you, Faith," he yelled from behind Vito's three contacts blocking his path.

"I've got one word for you, Harvey, LAWYER."

"I've got two for you, Faith. Prison Cell."

I slammed the door and leaned against it. Would this day never end? All this commotion was keeping us from our objective of returning Tessa and Rita to their father.

My earlier outburst was stupid, reckless, and I couldn't believe what I'd done. "With great powers comes great responsibility," came to mind. Fred was right. I was not prepared to live with the potency of The Alchemist's Dust. I doubted I ever would be.

Was I shown the dust to keep me so off-balance I couldn't concentrate on finding Tessa and Rita and solving whatever else was going on? Usually, my serial killer murdered his victims within a few hours. He'd had Tessa and Rita for more than a day now. And as far as I knew, he'd never taken two victims at once. This time, he also tried to kill Alinka.

"Tiffany, you know how The Alchemist's Dust is supposed to magnify things."

"Yes,"

"Let's hope it enhances our ability to read and process information. Let's heat some leftover pizza and dig in."

She looked at me with her head cocked and her weight firmly planted on her right hip. "So let me get this straight. You expect us to speed read through six boxes of books?"

"Yep, and our work is doubly hard because we each have to read all six, but cause what presented to you might not present to me."

Tiff grabbed two boxes of pizza from the fridge. "I've got an idea. Why don't you begin with the boxes that glowed pumpkin for you, and I'll start with the ones that glowed ruby? Maybe we won't have to go through them all."

"Sounds like a plan," I said, sticking two pizza plates in the dual microwaves.

Five minutes later, we sat at the breakfast bar with our lunch in front of us and old books beside us. "You do realize I haven't read from a physical book since picture books."

"Oh, just last year."

"Not funny. Then you are about to embark on a new experience. I remember so fondly begging Grams or Gramma to take me to the grocery store so I could crack open the cover of Tiger Beat Magainze or one of the lookalike rags. Turning out the lights at night and reading Nancy Drew with a flashlight under my tented covers. Carrying a thousand pounds of books from classroom to classroom. I've got to ask, does your backpack even contain books?"

"Notepads, my brush, and lip gloss."

"Start reading, Kiddo. Lives depend on us."

"Right. I know that. Which is probably why I'm rattling."

# CHAPTER 18

After finishing our pizza, Tiff and I moved outside onto the backyard deck and dug into our books. Sampson, Liberty, and Hudson, Arie and Tiff's dogs, chased each other around the obstacle course before jumping into Sampson's pool and then chasing again.

They were having a blast. I'd been reading for an hour. The Alchemist's Dust seemed to help with my reading speed. Hopefully, it worked for my retention speed as well. So far, I hadn't learned anything new about the case. I set some gardening and soil rotation books aside and added a few more names to the Abracadabra Lineage list. But nothing screamed clue in big, bold letters.

"Tiff, does lemonade sound good to you?"

"Yep, I was just thinking I needed to refill my ice water."

"Okay, a pitcher of lemonade coming right up." I swung my feet off the wicker footstool and watched Tiff untangle her legs. It would be so lovely to be that agile again. If I sat with my legs wrapped underneath me for an hour, I'd need a gallon of cooking oil to unstick them.

"I'll help," she said. "I need to give my butt a rest."

I walked to the fridge and Tiffany to the window. She peeked between the closed curtains. "Um, Faith. You need to see this."

"What now?" I came around the island and looked out the window. There was a sea of men outside the house. Vito's men stood on the front porch, facing the road. Four sheriff's department cars sat on the road's brim with the officers leaning against the cars facing the road.

Two men in suits leaned against a black SUV. Harvey talked with them.

"Tiff, have you gotten to The Shootout at the O.K. Corral in history yet?"

Tiff shook her head.

"Well, I'm positive it's a movie. We'll watch it sometime, but right now, I think we have a standoff at the Bracken House."

"What do we do?"

"We put the first aid kit on the front porch and get back to work on the books. If shooting starts, we hide under the back deck. When it stops, we call for paramedics."

"Works for me."

An hour later, Tiffany jumped out of her chair. "I've got something. I think I've got something." Punching the air with her arm, she twirled around twice.

I had to laugh. "Can you calm down long enough to tell me what it is?"

"This diary is written by Hannah Abbott. The first date is May 15, 1705. She was 17 years old. This book is almost three hundred years old and in remarkable shape. Hannah had been born in England, and then her family moved to France a few years later. They were forced to leave the country because of her parents' magic, and they bought passage on a ship coming to America. Two of her younger siblings died, leaving just her and her two parents.

"Her parents, reeling from their treatment in England and France, wanted to live as far from proper society as possible, so they made their way to the land they named Abracadabra. She says days after they arrived, other magic workers came family by family. She lists the names we already have, plus a few more, including the name Crane. If I'm reading this right, Mr. Crane was French, and his mother was part of the Potawatomi Native American tribe.

"Anyhow, they worked on their magic and became very powerful, and then, one day, the roof blew off the top of the alchemy building."

"Does she say why?"

"She writes the sun had disappeared behind the trees to the west. The winds pushed tree branches from side to side, and the magic was so heavy it pounded in my heart. Bang came from the thunder but not from the sky, and it was at least ten times more potent than any thunder I'd heard before. The roof of the building used for Alchemy flew into the air and disappeared out of sight. Prudence and I had been washing clothes using the new boil, suds, and blow spell. Pru was sucked up by the force, as were several others. A swirling rainbow followed the roof up out over our village. And twinkling lights of all colors hung in the air overhead for months.

"I never saw my friend again, nor the others who vanished, though I searched for her for weeks. The elders gathered and met for three days straight. The swirling rainbow continued to rain down upon us. Three days later, the elders gathered again and locked the dust in nine wooden boxes."

"Does it say anything about the curse?"

"Hold on. I'm getting there. She says, 'our families came here to practice our skills and ultimately turn anything we wanted into gold. Instead, what they found that day was the ability to draw from the Heavens and the ground's ultimate power, much like the stories of the Gods.'

"This post, or I guess they were called entries back then, is from a year later. She says, 'our colony has developed many things, and we have lived well. The soil has produced ten times the typical yield, and the sheep need to be sheered daily because they produce wool so fast. We harvest the corn weekly, and the apples rot, drop to the ground and grow trees so quickly that the roots and the crops fight for space. We are weary from developing spells to counter the effects of the other spells.' That's kind of sad."

"That makes sense."

"The families have not been getting along for some time now. Some have chosen to leave, settling in the lands around our settlement. They went on good terms and were allowed to take their magic dust and spells. However, many have walked away from the ways of magic. They hope for a simpler life."

"I can understand that," I said, squirming in my chair.

"However, tonight, three families' magic dust and spellbooks were seized from them, and they were cast out of the settlement by the elders, using a spell I've never heard before. Lester Crane glared at his brother and asked, 'you are my brother. How could you do this to your flesh and blood?'

"Lucas Crane clasped his brother's hand one more time. 'You are my brother—the most powerful wizard amongst us. Yet, your heart has gone black. You must go before evil infects us all.'

"Lester screamed at Lucas and all the settlers. 'I call up the wind, the rain, the thunder, and evil, to cast a curse upon you. In the seventh generation, after the oaks die and the natives cry, so to will you perish, and the power you covet will be returned to thee. Then darkness will fall upon the land, and evil will take her rightful stand.' And then he laughed so loud the trees bent over, and the ground shook."

"That's her last entry. Now, all we need to do is figure out when the Natives cried and the oaks died."

"Remind me to take you to a few museums around here. Of course, The Natives cried could mean anything but the Trail of Tears and the Trail of Death happened in the 1830s. I don't remember the exact years. The governments signed something like the Indian Removal Act, and Native Americans were forced off their land and across thousands of miles to reservations. Thousands died along the journey."

"That's horrible."

"Agreed. And we will plan a museum tour one of these days. But we can't change the past. What we can do is save Tessa and Rita. So if the Natives cried in the 1830s and back then, women had babies at fifteen," I pulled out my notepad. "The math works. My generation is the seventh generation after the Trail of Tears."

"No wonder Mr. Crane was so upset. Do you suppose that the bellowing we heard in the bookstore was Lester Crane, and do we know whether Howard is a descendant of Lester or Lucas?"

"I don't know. Crane wasn't one of the names we had. My gut says, Lucas. Howard's family has been here a long time. If they were descendants of Lester, I doubt they'd be allowed to stay."

"Maybe Lester and his family went to live with The Potawatomi," Tiff offered.

"I don't know enough about historical Native American culture to hazard a guess."

"What we do know is The Alchemist's Dust is super potent. Lester Crane was the most powerful. We know from Hannah's account they confiscated his dust. What if the elders used his dust against him to cast him and his family as far away as possible? But at that moment, Lester also used the dust to fire the curse."

"What if they didn't get all his Alchemist's Dust? What if he had some hidden?" Tiff asked. "Or. Okay," she said with one eye closed and her head cocked.

"What if somehow Lester's being or persona or ghost or whatever the heck we are going to call it is what bellowed? What if he is the mirror opposite of The Lighter?"

"Now we are getting deep. So the Lighter is a good witch, and Lester Crane is a wicked witch."

"Yes."

"That would make Lester Crane the original Murker," Tiffany said. She picked up a stick Hudson had dropped before him and flung it across the dog pen.

"I think we need to go visit Trixie."

# CHAPTER 19

There are two ways to pop into the In-Between. Take your whole body or just your essence. Just because we could, we left the boys outside and took our entire bodies into the In-Between to see Trixie.

"Faith, Tiffany, I'm so glad to see you. Vito was here a few minutes ago and said they had you on ice."

"They do. One question, can Vito's contacts stop us from entering the in-between?"

Trixie smiled. "I love the way you think, Faith. They'd have to hang out in the In-Between, waiting to block you. That requires a great deal of energy. And it sounds like their energy is needed in the physical capacity. If they do, surround yourself with mental magic dust, say 'Ivan,' and snap your fingers twice. You'll be invisible and can jump past them. But Vito's contacts are there to protect you. Remember that."

"We can go invisible?" Tiff asked.

"Yes, you can."

"Grams, when we come out, will we still be invisible?"

"No, you'll be fine, except sometimes the landing is harder. I don't know why. It just is. I landed on my nose once. Had to wear a bandage on it for days."

"Good to know. How are you feeling?"

"I'm doing okay. You should see my physical therapist. He has buns stronger than steel. I'd so love to get my hands on them, but he's quick."

"You are the best, Grams."

"I am, aren't I. Tell that to your grandfather. But you didn't escape to hear about the hotties in my world, and it is safer for you back home, so tell me what's on your mind?"

"Tiffany found an old diary written by Hannah Abbot. She talks about the early days in the Abracadabra settlement and the curse. The curse was cast by Lester Crane. Aside from Howard, does that name ring a bell?"

"You do know I had brain surgery yesterday. But it does. It's time I gave you access to the Lighter's Archives."

I looked at her. There's an archive. All this time, we'd been running around, and there was an archive.

"Don't give me that face, Faith. I didn't know that's where this was going, and before you and Tiffany have access, you both have huge decisions to make."

"And what is that decision?"

"You have to commit five hundred percent to being a Lighter. You can never, ever walk away from the ways of a Lighter, and you must be fully committed to teaching people the ways of a lighter."

"Teaching how?" Tiffany asked with brows raised.

"First, you can never denounce or bad mouth witches, magic, alchemist, etc. Best practice is never to denounce or bad-mouth anyone because we all possess magic at some level. If someone asks you if you are a witch, a magician, etc., you must say yes. There are creative ways to answer questions without answering that I can teach you, but life is not always easy."

"What else?" I asked. "One of the things I've learned these last few weeks is there is always more."

"You are correct. You must live as a Lighter. You know how on *Bewitched,* Samantha was always trying to live a normal life. Once I've given you full Lighter status, you must devote a part of your time to perfecting magic. You can still run your businesses, but one-quarter of your time must be devoted to perfecting your magic. I can teach you creative ways to meld the two. For instance, have you ever seen me clean the house?"

I thought back to my childhood. "No, Mom, I can't say I did."

"Did you ever see either of your grandmothers clean the house?"

"No. They made Arie and me."

"Because we were trying to keep you out of the family business."

"Anything else we need to know?"

"I was getting there, Faith. I just had surgery. Yes, the archives aren't normal archives."

"Of course not."

She frowned at my response. "Don't be rude." Her temper started a slow boil. I could see it in the set of her jaw, and her color was draining. We needed to get out of there and let her rest.

"You know how some people think the government is spying on them? Well, we are way better. When you enter the archives, you can see everything in what you call 3D today. You'll know if those pants made your butt look fat. You'll see what those brownies did to your waist. There is no hiding from the truth once you enter the archives. It can be a brutal place to go. I urge you to take some time to consider your decisions, and Tiffany, you need to talk it over with your father."

"But we don't have time. Every second the serial killer has Tessa and the others, the more likely we are to find their bodies," I said.

"Right, there's a present on your coffee table waiting for you. Fred will help you work it. If Fred gets too bossy, tell him you will cut some onions. That'll shut him up."

"Now, I should probably rest, and you should get back. Vito's contacts are the best at what they do. Pretty soon, they'll figure out you escaped and come looking for you."

# CHAPTER 20

Something caused me to take Tiffany's hand before we slipped into the In-Between. Every time I thought I had this magic thing handled, some new piece of information surfaced and sent me in a new befuddled direction. There were times I missed my old life. I understood Chi. I was a master balancer. Very few could match my skills, but boy howdy, this magic stuff upended my world.

I'd just brought both feet into the In-Between when Tiffany flinched and squeezed my hand.

"Hello, Dear Faith. So good to meet you here in this space. Your powers have grown since the last time we met. I am impressed." He stood right in front of me. It's hard to explain the In-Between. For me, it's like a narrow electric blue tube with a baby blue lighting system inside it. There is hardly room for two people, and I'd never passed anyone before. I wasn't exactly sure how to get by him. But I would.

"Get out of our way, Upton."

"What a lovely niece you have, Faith. What's your name, Darlin?" He reached his hand toward Tiff's face.

I smacked his arm away. "Don't you dare touch her."

"What are you going to do to me, Faith? You're good, but the Mask is not here. All you have is your flimsy magic dust. Did you know a skilled magician can turn your dust against you?"

"I'm warning you, Upton, get out of my way, or I'll plant my knee in your favorite little bitty appendage."

He laughed.

"Upton, what is your problem? What do you want from me? You've got both Alinka and Rita fawning over you. Why me? You know I have nothing but contempt for you."

"Ah, but it's always the one that got away, my dear."

"See, that's what I don't get. I was never there. I have no interest in living in your world. None whatsoever?"

I tried to maneuver Tiff and myself around him. He shifted his weight to the left, stopping me.

"Perhaps you have something I need."

"Such as."

"In good time, my dear."

He reached to touch my face. I flung my magic dust at him.

He reached for me again. My dust seemed to make him stronger. I kicked where it would do the most good. He swayed to the side, and my foot connected with his knee. He lunged forward.

"Dust, Ivan," Tiffany said. Her grip on my hand tightened. Her fingers snapped twice. We flipped and flopped and twisted and rolled. It was the most active flight through the In-Between yet. Usually, one foot landed and then the next. Not this time. My butt crashed hard onto the roof of my house with both feet sticking straight up in the air. Tiff planted beside me. Thank goodness we were both wearing pants.

"Thanks, Tiff."

"No problem. While you were fighting with Upton, I had the opportunity to sprinkle some of my dust, and I called upon The Alchemist's Dust. Although, I think I used too much. My butt hurts." She said, rubbing her behind. "What is that Upton guy's problem? We've met a lot of freaks on our magical path. I'm hoping for some hot wizards soon."

"Sane wizards would be good." I rocked to a sitting position.

"What are you two doing up there?" One of Vito's contacts yelled.

"We needed some sun."

"Do I need to come up there and help you down?" He asked in my grandfather's-backside-whooping voice. Stash and Eagle must be on break. I liked them better.

"Is there a way down?" Tiffany asked.

"Yes, remember Vito is a mob boss. Follow me."

We crawled a few feet to the backside of the roof before I opened what looked like a window, and we descended the ladder to the attic.

"Now, let's go find Fred and the dogs and see what's inside the mysterious package Trixie said is waiting for us."

# CHAPTER 21

Tiffany let Sampson, Liberty, and Hudson outside. I walked into the living room to find Fred sitting on top of a box with giant red and orange floral wrapping paper and a green bow Fred had pushed to the side.

"What?" Fred said with his bunny eyes narrowed. "It was in my way. It scratches. I prefer satin. That stuff feels like rope."

"Will you get off of it long enough for me to open it?"

He stretched. "I will. Read the instructions while I go outside to poop. Don't try to work it without me."

I rubbed my hands together. Did I really want to open the box? Maybe I should permanently close the lid on this magic stuff and live like an average person. Life had been easier. A great deal easier.

"You haven't opened it yet," Tiffany said, coming into the room.

"No, I was waiting for you."

She looked at me sideways. "No, you weren't. You are stalling. Open the box and let's see what's inside."

Tiffany could be the most mature person in the room, and then she turned into a little kid. I lifted the lid on the box and gasped. Inside was an eight-inch crystal ball filled with lilac smoke sitting on a base of gold filigree. The insides swirled.

"It's beautiful," Tiffany said.

"I was thinking majestic."

"That too. What are we supposed to do with it?"

I cradled my hands around it and raised it while Tiffany moved the box to the floor. After lowering it to the coffee table, I sat back and admired it.

"Fred says we need to wait for him to work it."

"Arie's cat is demanding, but Fred is the bossiest and mouthiest animal I've ever met," Tiff said.

Mr. Mouthy Rabbit pawed the French Doors, and I let the dogs and him in.

"Okay, Fred, how do we work this thing? I've seen this in movies." Tiffany asked, almost jumping out of her skin with enthusiasm.

"This is not a toy. This is a very sophisticated magical apparatus. And it doesn't work as you see on television. "

Fred needed to lighten up. "Fred, we understand. Tell us what we need to do first."

"Let me set your expectations. You can't just ask it questions and have a 3-D image appear inside." He flipped his ears and shook his head. "I don't know why they didn't deliver two balls. Usually, the ball is tuned to the energy of one person. But we won't get that advanced today, so both of you using it should work for now. Whatever, The Lighter can always recalibrate it."

He seemed a little disoriented. Fred obviously had a specific way of doing things, and he didn't enjoy disruptions.

"Fred, time is of the essence here. Just give us enough information to use this thing.

"Yes, yes, I've got it. Close your eyes and focus your attention on your third eye between your eyebrows. Think of Tessa and Rita. Faith, you know them, so form a picture. Tiffany, focus on their names. Now, each of you put your right hand on the ball. When you have a sense of them clearly in mind, open your eyes and gaze into the ball."

Fred placed his paw upon the ball. I took a few moments to sort through the clutter in my mind and find their images. Tessa had depth and was kind. Rita was a mouthy, spoiled, but talented brat who hadn't grown up.

When I felt I had them anchored in my mind, I opened my eyes and gazed into the ball. At first, I didn't see anything. The smoke inside swirled. Tiffany's hand covered the other side. I waited. The only sound was the water running in Sampson's dog bowl fountain.

Five minutes we sat there at least. Was I doing this wrong? Was I supposed to see something? Was this a trick? This was a significant waste of time when we needed to be out looking for the two women. This magic stuff was just a major distraction. Why was I even participating in it?

And then, a vision of a barn came to me: a big, two-story barn with weathered red siding——the real thing. It sat on top of a cement base. Some of the concrete blocks were exposed. A metal rooster swung around in circles. A badge floated inside the ball. Tessa, Rita, Amy Prescott, and Jenna Jasmine sat tied to wooden beams. I'd seen that barn. Where?

"I think I've got something," I finally said.

"Me too," Tiffany agreed. "You go first."

I told her my vision. "What did you see?"

"Not that. I saw Howard Crane. Digging frantically out behind the Magic Factory. He'd stop and wipe the sweat from his head, fall to the ground, cry, and repeat."

"Fred, what did you see?"

"Oh, I fell asleep. I've never been good at working these things."

Great, when time was of the essence, I thought. We had a Crystal Ball dud as a teacher.

"I'm not a dud. I told you how to do it, and you figured it out."

Tiffany fell backward into her chair. "Do you know how many old red barns there are in this county? I'm going to call Jenna and make sure she's alright. Then maybe we can escape again and look for Howard behind the Magic Factory. We'd better take some water. He looked pale."

Tiffany got up and went out on the back deck to make her phone call. Jenna and Tiffany had been through a significant ordeal when they first met. They basically saved each other's lives. Tiff and I were close, but she shared a special bond with Jenna I couldn't understand. I hoped they remained tight once Jenna moved to Abracadabra. Sometimes distance is the key to a long-term relationship, which is probably how I stuck with Max for so long.

# CHAPTER 22

Tiffany came inside with a long face and dropped her phone on the couch. "Jenna's voicemail said she was driving now and to leave a message."

"Well, that makes sense. She's probably got a million things to finish before she moves down here."

"Yeah, probably," Tiffany said, falling onto the couch. "What time is Blake getting released?"

"7 Pm. He has to stay for ten hours after his test."

Tiffany looked at the clock. "So we've got time to run over to the Magic Factory and see if Howard is there. Then we can come back here and scour Google Maps for the barn you saw in your vision."

I popped the tab on a root beer. "Okay, how do we get out of here? We've got an army outside the door, so we can't take the car. If we slip into the In-Between, we risk another encounter with Upton. How do we get from here to there?"

"Good point. We could make a run for it."

"Yeah, that won't work. Those men are highly trained. We aren't. Fred, do you have any ideas?"

"You are both witches. You could just use your invisibility screens and walk right past them. But remember, when you leave this house, you leave the protections in place unless, of course, I come with you. With Upton and a serial killer running around, I believe we need to take the dogs. And I refuse to hop that far, so one of you will need to carry me."

Tiffany rolled her eyes. "Will you ride in a backpack?"

"As long as my head is sticking out."

A thought crossed my mind. "Tiffany, upstairs in the spare bedroom closet are a couple of backpacks and some old leashes. Rather than us going through Google Maps, I'll call Blister. He's working for Dad now. What would take us hours to complete; he can work his magic and do in minutes. I'll have him find the possible barns from my vision."

"Sound good." She ran up the stairs. I dialed Blister.

"Hello, my sexy queen. What can the Amazing Blister do for you today?"

I told him about my vision. "Your pops has me working on an urgent matter. Bout to wrap it up in fifteen. Your request is my next command, oh great one.

"Thank you, oh master keyboarder."

"Don't I know it."

"Oh, and can you see if any of the barns are or were owned by law enforcement officers or have been crime scenes? Something like that."

"You know it. Blister is on the job."

He disconnected us.

Tiffany came into the living room with leashes and a backpack. Come on, dogs, it's time for an excursion.

"Make sure you have a huge supply of magic dust with you," I said to Tiff.

"Refilled while I was upstairs."

I held the backpack open and allowed Fred to climb in and settle himself.

"So, Tiffany used The Ivan Magic Spell to make us invisible and save us from Upton in the In-Between. Do we use the same spell to get to the Magic Factory?"

"I'll work the invisibility screen. We've got quite a large party to keep behind it, and I saw how you two landed last time. I'm afraid I might end up in the middle of Moon Lake if either of you two were in charge. Once the Magic Factory opens, you both need to buckle down and work on your spell casting."

Tiffany's eyes rolled again.

"Young lady, keep doing that, and your eyes will be permanently rotating."

"Fred, are you this tough on all your students?"

He thumped his feet inside the backpack, which hurt my back. "Lives aren't usually on the line when I teach."

"I understand how we can get by the sheriff's deputies and the feds, but how will we get past Vito's men? Won't they detect our magic?"

"Let's go out the backdoor. Vito's men are focused on the feds and police."

Fred made some gurgling sounds I'd never heard come from a rabbit, and we all walked out the back gate, around the yard, and started toward the factory.

Today was a beautiful spring day. I was anxious to start planting. It had only been a couple of days since I last saw my nursery stock, but I missed stopping by Nothing Fancy and checking on them. All this magic stuff was exhausting. It was nice to work with the plants and let the dirt ground me.

There was so much work to get the building and my business ready. The last thing we needed was someone dying on the grounds.

I thought about Tessa, Rita, and Amy Prescott. How were they doing? How was their father holding up? No one had said much about Alinka's condition. I assumed she was still alive. I hadn't heard anything to negate that belief. Arie and Vito had been scarce. I missed being included in the physical investigation. Chasing down magic was infinitely more complicated.

My phone rang. It was Arie.

"I'm at your house with Pete and Link. Is Tiffany with you, and are you safe?" He said each word in slow even beats. The flames from his anger radiated through the phone.

"We are safe."

"Where are you, and why did you leave your protection?"

"It's my dad, right?" Tiffany said. "He's hot."

I nodded and put him on speaker.

"We had a lead."

"Since I'm talking to you on the phone, I know you understand how phones work."

"Perhaps. Meet us behind the Magic Factory, but be quiet about it."

He ended the call.

"He's going to yell at us for a week straight," Tiffany said.

"Yeah, I believe you are correct."

# CHAPTER 23

Fred made us un-invisible as Arie's SUV came into view. I assumed Pete and Link were in the vehicle, following him.

Arie slammed on the brakes. "Get in," he ordered. "I'm taking you back to the house."

"No," I put my hand on his shoulder. "We may have a lead. Let us check it out and then we'll go invisible again and sneak back in."

He turned the corner sharply into the factory's lane. "You know you have two details to keep you safe. Not so you can practice your spells."

"I am sorry we worried you, but you put us in charge of the magical investigation, and this is where it led us."

He slammed on the brakes at the back of the parking lot. "Don't turn this around on me. I thought putting you two in charge of magic would keep you safe. I should have known better. Do you know what went through my mind when I walked into the house and couldn't find you? I was the most scared I've ever been in my life. And I can't get a hold of Jenna. Her phone keeps saying she's driving. You'd think she'd stop once in a while to check her messages. Women. Why do you have to all be so darn difficult?"

He opened his door, climbed out, and slammed it.

"I think he's ticked," Tiffany said.

"Yeah, just a little. At least we have Fred and the dogs to protect us."

Fred thumped me from the backpack. "Don't include me in this. I'm an innocent rabbit along for the ride."

"You said the back," Arie yelled. "I'm going around back. Try to keep up, or I'll drag the two of you."

In response, Liberty barked.

"You be quiet. I know you are on their side." He stomped around the building.

Pete and Link joined Tiffany and me. "He'll get over it in about twenty years," Pete said.

"You two scared the crap out of him," Link said.

We started around behind the building. "That wasn't our intention. We had a lead and needed to follow it."

"Well, lead on, ladies," Pete indicated with his arm for us to go ahead. I let her go ahead since it was Tiffany's vision, and she'd had prior experience with the buildings behind the factory. I knew she and Jenna had been held captive in one of these structures. That's where they met. No one talked about it much, but I sensed it had been a harrowing experience for her and ended with Tiff losing her mother and the father who had raised her. And she'd come to live with Aire.

From what I'd deduced, Trixie and Vito had been in her life for quite a long time, but Anita never wanted Arie to know he had a daughter until the end, when she sensed she was in trouble and could be killed. That was just supposition on my part. No one had told me all the details. How Jenna Jasmine had become part of the mix was still a mystery.

We rounded another building, and there, between two out-house-sized buildings, lay Howard Crane on the ground with a shovel in his hand. He was breathing and semi-conscious. He'd dug several holes in the earth and cleared a kiddie-pool-sized dirt area in the center. Tiffany pulled a water bottle from the backpack she'd prepared for Howard and tossed it to Arie, who held Howard's head off the ground.

Link took off his T-shirt and had Tiff wet it. He wiped Howard's face. "Howard, what are you doing here?" Link asked.

"I'm digging holes."

"I can see that. Why?"

"I'm looking for the Lighter's wand. It's gone. Someone stole it."

"Okay, Howard, be still for a few minutes and take small sips," Link said.

Arie pulled Pete to the side. "What do you think?" He asked Pete. "You two know Howard better. Is he delirious?"

I scanned the area. And then took my time taking in the sights. The earth was a different color in several places. Careful not to get too far away from the group, I wandered over to the first discolored soil patch. When I pushed my toe on the spot, it sank a bit. Someone or thing had dug a hole, probably with a hand-held post-hole digger, and then filled the dirt back in. It happened several weeks ago. Weeds had already started to root.

"Faith," Arie yelled. "Get back over here. Haven't you caused enough trouble today?"

"Look, I'm sorry we scared you, but quit being mad and come look at this."

He racked his hand through his hair so hard a few strands fell from his fingers and stomped toward me. "What?"

"I think Howard is right. Look at all those spots. Someone dug around here. Maybe three months ago."

He dropped down and inspected the soil. "Maybe a little before that. It's hard to tell because of the winter season. The ground didn't freeze around here until a few weeks before you came home."

He put his hand on my elbow, and we walked from spot to spot. Each was the same. A hole had been dug and then haphazardly filled in. "It does appear someone was digging around looking for something. But how do we know it wasn't Howard?"

I turned back to look at Howard. "You know how secretive Howard is. He would have filled these holes, so they were perfect, and no one could tell."

"Let's ask him about them, and then we need to call medics and have him checked out."

When we returned, Howard was able to sit upright. "You found the holes," he said. "I need to tell you something. We haven't much time."

"Okay, tell us," I said.

"But before I can tell you, you must all agree to follow the ways of The Lighter. I cannot divulge the secrets if you won't agree. And once you agree, magic must always be a part of your lives, and you must embrace it. There's no turning back. If you denounce magic, bad things will happen. You all are descendants of The Lighters. That's why the elders worked so hard to group you in one place and unite you. Anyone unwilling to pledge to The Lighter Traditions must walk away now."

What the heck. If I turned away, I knew magic would haunt me until I accepted my fate. "I'm in," I said.

"Me too," said Tiff.

"Yeah, alright. I'm in if it will stop the curse," Arie agreed.

Pete and Link looked at one another. "Yeah."

"Good. You know about the books, the magic dust, the Alchemist's Dust, and all of it is powerful, but the Lighter's Wand ties all those pieces together. And unlocks all the spells and magic developed within the walls of the Magic Factory. You'll still need the missing decryption codes, The Mask of Bleudorf, the rest of the Alchemist's Dust, and a few more surprises to unlock the total power, but The Lighter's Want is the most important piece. When Lester Crane cast his curse, his brother created a fail-safe. I'll tell you the story later, but you need one female from the seventh generation after the Natives Cry of each of the Seven Families of The Lighter's Council to unlock the powers. Plus, one female member from The Lighter's Circle. The seven families are The Collins, The Jasmines, The Montaignes, The Brackens, The Prescotts, the Abbots, and The Cranes."

So that explains why they took Rita and Tessa. They are the Montaigne line. Upton has been after Faith as both a Bracken and Montaigne. Amy Prescott is missing. This means Monique, Sydney, and Elle Collins are in danger, but we don't have an Abbott or a female Crane.

"Yes, we do," Howard said. "Grace Collins is a Crane from her mother's side, which means Sydney, Elle, and Monique are Cranes and Collins. And Tiffany, your mother descends from the Abbot line."

"Right, but Tiffany is the wrong generation," Arie said.

Howard frantically shook his head. "No, the Abbots have always been slow to marry. She is part of the Seventh Generation."

"But then, how do Pete and Link fit in?" I asked, needing to understand and not wanting to leave them out.

"Due to tribal rules, the Chief never took part in the Lighter's Council, but he was part of the community until he was forced to leave by the government."

"Okay, but we still need the Lighter's Circle. Who are they?" Pete asked.

"We don't know. It is believed the Lighter's Circle was outside of Abracadabra. The circle consisted of the greatest magicians of the time and communicated telepathically. We are still hunting for that part of the legend in the Archives."

"Great," said Arie. "And this is all legend, so how much of it is true remains to be seen."

"But the killer thinks it's real," Pete said. "That's what's important right now."

"We'll worry about the backstory later," Pete said. "Right now, we need to get Howard to a hospital. You two back to the house, and we need to find Jenna."

Arie called Jenna one more time. "No answer. That's it. I'm pinging her phone."

"You know, it might be faster if you call Blister. He works beyond the laws."

"Good thinking."

"He might not answer for you. I dialed and handed the phone to Arie.

"This isn't Hot Lips," Arie said. "It's her brother. I need you to ping a phone. I need a location. Stat." Arie walked away from us. Pete had called for paramedics. The sirens were in the distance.

"You realize that as soon as the sirens pass my house, Harvey's men will be here, looking for us. Fred, you need to make us invisible again, and we need to hightail it for the house."

"Right," said Fred. "We'll see you gentleman back at the ranch."

# CHAPTER 24

Fred was much better at landings than Tiff. He pulled us in and through the In-Between, and we arrived at home with Tiff sitting on the couch, me resting in my favorite chair, and the dogs chasing through the obstacle course. Fred lounged on the pillow beside Tiffany.

The ambulance's taillights hadn't cleared the road outside when Harvey marched around the sheriff's cars and stood at the foot of my front porch steps yelling at Vito's men. I couldn't make out much of the conversation, but his voice's tone was annoying, so I got up, opened the front door, and stood at the entrance.

"What is the problem, Special Agent?"

"I needed to know you were still inside the building."

"Really? Where would I go? Apparently, you haven't been able to convince a judge I have the power to be in two places at once, or you'd be in here arresting me."

"Faith, I know you have all four women. Where are you hiding them? This can't end well for you. Come outside and let me take you in."

"Lawyer," I said, closing the door.

"Harvey," said four women. "Who else has been taken?" Tiffany asked. All the color drained from her face.

I dialed Pete. "Hey, Harvey just accused me of having all four women. Are Sydney, Elle, and Monique all right?"

"Yeah, I just hung up with them to answer your call. The trio, plus Lois and Grace, are all hunkered down. Lois has her shotgun and rifle laying across the arms of her scooter."

"Jenna," Tiff cried. "The killer must have Jenna."

"Blister tracked Jenna's phone," Pete said. "I am afraid I have worrisome news."

"Oh, no." Tiffany wept.

"Maybe you should take me off speaker," Pete said.

Tiff glared at me. "Don't you dare. I need to hear this. Jenna is my friend. We saved each other's lives."

"Go on, Pete."

"Jenna's phone last pinged at a truck stop on County Road 17, just south of the bypass in Elkhart. Arie and Link are on their way. We don't know anything yet. Blister gave Arie the information on the barns. A crew of Vito's men and I are checking them out. We're rolling up on one now."

"Thanks."

Tiffany burst into tears. Her body shook with force. I wrapped her in my arms. "Jenna has the best team anyone could ask for looking for her. They'll find her."

"That's what we thought about Tessa and Rita, and they're still missing."

"You heard Pete. They are hitting every possible target. It's just going to take a little more time."

"Time they may not have."

"Oh, they'll have time. Whoever is behind this needs them, two members of the Collins Trio, and you and me. Until they have us all, they need to keep the others alive. And just because they have us doesn't mean we'll know how to work the wand. Like, do we all have to touch it at once? Is there a spell we need to recite? We'll find them."

Tiffany continued to weep. I didn't blame her. In fact, I wanted to join her, but the stakes were too high.

"Fred, help me out here. Does the killer have Jenna? There has to be some magic trick you can pull out of a hat. And where is Vito? And where is that darn Lighter? It pops in and out at the most inopportune times. Where is it when we need it?"

"Vito and The Lighter are with Trixie."

Fear instantly penetrated my body. "Is she alright?"

"She's fine. They are working at the highest levels. Levels you are not ready to understand."

"Okay, well, give me something I can understand to do?"

Fred sat on his back feet. And placed a bunny paw on my hand. "I believe we need to start at the beginning. From the time you think the holes were dug and work our way backward, looking for patterns."

"Right, good idea. Let me grab my whiteboard."

Fred hopped off the pillow. "Why don't we go into your office, Faith? Let the men outside deal with each other and leave their energy at the door."

"Right, good thinking, Fred."

I took a picture of everything on the whiteboard and erased it.

"What happened first?" Fred asked. Fred is the bossiest animal I've ever met, but right now, I was glad he was here, helping me stay grounded. The dogs had positioned themselves around us. If someone came through the front door, they'd have to go through them.

"Okay, so we are guessing the holes were dug five to six months ago."

"My mother and the dad I grew up with were killed by Lucinda Jasmine five months ago, and I moved in with Arie. Vito and Trixie moved home about the same time."

I thought back to L.A. It all started there. "I lost my reflection and found the first body about that same time. Then I went to the Bahamas, where I met Tessa, Rita, and Alinka and used the Mask of Bleudorf to defend myself against Upton and Max. Then I went to Spirit Island to recover, and then I kept finding bodies until I was forced to come back to Abracadabra, where I met Blake."

"Blake, OMG, I forgot about Blake. He should be here by now. What's happened to Blake?"

I grabbed my phone. Fred, who had left the room for a moment, hopped back inside. "Relax, he's outside talking to the deputies. I assume they are briefing him."

I swallowed, and the tightness in my throat and shoulders dissipated. "Oh, thank goodness."

"Mr. Raymont was killed, and Harvey was shot outside the restaurant." I popped the cap on the dry-erase marker and listed everything.

"Someone put the box of books into your moving pod, and Shayla stole it. We freed Alex Houston." Tiffany said.

"Then Lisa Blooms' sister Bailey was shot, and Lisa shot Blake while stealing the encryption code, but she doesn't have the books. We do," I said. "Gerald Landcaster came into town and warned us about the Murkers."

"The Peacock came to town," Tiffany said, referencing Able, who now worked for my father, "and Blister went to work for Grandpa too. Only he doesn't live here yet."

"Alinka Albertson was beaten, and someone kidnapped Tessa Johnson, Rita Rocca, Amy Prescott, and Jenna Jasmine."

"Faith, don't forget to add many members of the seventh generation have been murdered or died in strange ways over the years."

I wrote the names of the people we'd lost from my high school years on the board and added, "Feds outside in a standoff with Vitos' men."

In truth, there was one car with two federal agents. Harvey came and went.

Then my hand wrote. "Harvey frames Faith for the murders." I stared at that statement for a minute.

"Don't forget now you have Upton, Harvey, and Max in town," Fred said, bringing me back to the conversation.

"I've got a question," Tiffany said. "How did Harvey know Jenna was missing before we did? And how did he tie in Amy Prescott? She doesn't live around here, and unless he knew about the legend, why would he tie her in? Hundreds of people disappear daily, so how could he tie Amy to you?"

I put down the marker and hugged myself. "How is he justifying the man hours for those agents to sit outside my door when I have airtight alibis? At the time of the murders, I was oblivious to my magic. I can't believe Harvey's bosses are buying the two places at once things. So how's that all working? Did anyone check and make sure they are FBI Agents?"

Fred thumbed his feet. "Oh shucks. Probably not. Harvey was with them when they arrived, so no one checked because they accompanied Special Agent Wallbanger."

Tiffany handed me another root beer. "Faith, make a new column for suspects and put Harvey, Max, Upton, and Howard's names under that."

"What makes you suspect Howard?" I asked.

"There's something wrong with that guy. And when Jenna and I were captured, this guy Ace was running around in the maze. Ace and Howard are connected somehow. I can feel it."

I grabbed my phone. "Hello," Blister said.

"What no, Hey, sexy queen."

"I was making sure you were you. Don't ever again hand your phone to your brother."

"Sorry bout that. Time was critical. I need you to do me a favor."

"What can I do for my lady?"

"I need you to tell me where Special Agent Wallbanger, Max, and Upton were at the time of each of the West Coast Murders and the last couple of days. Were any of their phones near the Magic Factory maybe five or six months ago? And one more thing, get me whatever information you can find on Howard Crane of Moon Lake. I'd be surprised if you find much."

"Consider it done, sexy bottom. I'll hit you back in seconds."

# CHAPTER 25

S ampson knocked me to the side as I pushed the end call button. He raced to the front door with Liberty and Hudson on his tail. All three dogs barked at full volume. The door opened. "Get in the corner behind the door," Fred ordered.

"It's me." Blake's voice yelled. "I could use a little help with the canine welcoming party."

"Stay put," Fred ordered. "Let me double-check. Dark energy might be mimicking Blake's voice." He jumped off the desk and hopped to the door. Tiffany and I huddled in the corner.

"Anybody here?" Blake asked.

"It's Blake," Fred said.

I walked from the office and hugged him. "Sorry about the welcome. We are a little on edge."

"As you should be." He said, resting against the couch back. "I've been in contact with Pete, Link, and Arie."

"Please tell me they've found Jenna?" Tiffany said.

"How about we sit down, and I'll tell you what I know?" He was recovering from a gunshot wound, and here I was making him stand. I was losing my mind and manners all at one time. "We were working in the office. Let me get my rolling chair, and I'll push you there. Unless you'd like to lie down."

"Rolling chair sounds great."

Tiffany had already grabbed it. "Here you go." She pushed him in front of the whiteboard while I moved the footstool under his legs.

"Okay, now, what do we know about Jenna?"

He paused and looked at Tiff. "Tiffany, your dad wanted to be the one to give you the news, but you are asking. We found Jenna's car in a truck stop parking lot. The driver's side was a mess, indicating she tried to use everything in the console to defend herself. There was minimal blood."

"How minimal?" I asked. Tiff sat with her legs forced together and her arms hugging herself. She rocked back and forth.

"Cat-scratch amount of blood. From what I understand, they need her alive. And it wasn't her blood type."

"Were BMC and Bugsy with her?" Tiffany asked.

"No, she wanted to be here to wait with Arie during Trixie's surgery."

"So she's been missing as long as Tessa and Jenna," I said. "Did you loop Harvey in on her disappearance?"

He grimaced and rubbed his chin. "Aside from my inner circle and you all, no one knows Jenna is missing. She appears as a Jane Doe from an anonymous tip. Why do you ask?"

"Faith got in a yelling match with Harvey not long ago. He said four girls were missing. How would he know that? And Alinka was beaten. Not murdered. The police found her, so why would Harvey be alerted?"

"Good point, Tiff," Blake said. "We've searched every red barn in the county and are now starting to search barns in the surrounding areas as well as barns that are brown, or black, or have lost the color over time. So far, we've come up empty."

"Monique Collins and her network of psychics took a run at this, and they came up with the same red barn image."

Blake rubbed his leg. The man should rest. Not solve crime.

"This may be crazy, and I have no basis other than my gut. But we've got the Alchemist's Dust, or supposedly we can draw upon it."

"Right," said Blake. "So it takes seven to use the wand, but I wonder what five of us working together with the dust could do. What if Sydney, Monique, Elle, Tiffany, and I were all in the same room, and we called upon the dust? We know we can't unlock all the secrets, but maybe we could get the crystal ball to give us a better picture."

Blake didn't say anything. He seemed to be studying the whiteboard.

"I think it's a great idea. At least we could try rather than sit here helpless," Tiffany said.

"Um," Blake scratched the side of his chin. "The logic is sound, but it's risky. Putting you all in one spot could give the killer what he wants. Scoop you everybody, at once. Or grab you in transport."

"Are they watching The Collins Spread?"

"Not that we know. I need to talk to Pete, Link, and Arie. Do you suppose you ladies could make me a burger and some fries? The hospital food lacked flavor."

"Come on, Tiff. He's trying to get rid of us."

# CHAPTER 26

Tiffany chopped lettuce while I grilled three burgers and nuked some fries. My phone beeped. It was Blister.

"Feng Shui Witch here. No men in the room."

"Hey, Darlin, I've got some news. Twenty-two weeks ago, Special Agent Harvey Wallbanger arrested Upton Crescent's old business partner, Randy Carmichael, in Michigan City, Indiana. The charge was trafficking exotic animals. But then evidence went missing, and the guy never went to jail. I've not been able to find a trace of him since. Two days after Randy's arrest, Harvey had lunch at a diner in Crumstown, Indiana, with a woman I can't identify. The image is too blurry, and Upton paid for their meals. He purchased a post-hole digger at a home store twenty minutes later. His phone turned off after that."

"What about Max?"

"Except for your vacation in The Bahamas and his trip to meet Tessa the other day, Max hasn't left L.A."

"And Upton?"

"The Magic rat is harder to track. His phone is seldom on, and he rarely uses a credit card. However, Max makes regular calls to a number in the Bahamas, and so does your buddy Able Heinz. Vito has had me up on Able's phone for a while now."

"Who hired Able when he worked at Crescent?"

"Sleeping Ugly."

"I take it that's Lenora."

"You know it, babe.

"Well, that would make sense. He is her type. Did she show him any special treatment?"

"While Cash was working late at the office, Able helped Lenora on several projects at the Crescent residence."

"What about Howard?"

"You are right, other than property records on a farm in Moon Lake and utility bills. He has no digital footprint. He doesn't collect Social Security or Medicare. He's a ghost."

"Thanks, Blister."

"That's all for now, Honey Bun. Blister out."

Tiffany finished flipping the burgers. Blake pushed himself from my office. "None of us think it's a good idea to put all of you in the same room. However, Vito is having the same crystal balls delivered to the Collins Spread and another one for here. Once the balls are delivered, which should be in about fifteen minutes, you ladies can go into the office and Zoom with the Collins Trio. Vito, Trixie, and Howard believe that will work. They'll be on Zoom too. Not Howard. He doesn't Zoom." Blake rolled his eyes.

"Howard is an acquired taste," I agreed. "Well, eat up, and then we can get down to business."

# CHAPTER 27

Thirty minutes later, we sat in front of our computers with our crystal balls, chatting with the Collins Trio and Trixie and Vito. Blake sat outside the door. The dogs lay on the back deck with their butts against the glass, protecting us from anyone who might attack from the south.

"I'm not much of a crystal ball reader," Monique said, "but I have used them in the past. I gave Syd and Elle a crash course. Mrs. Bracken, why don't you guide us?"

Trixie beamed in response. "I have always loved crystal balls. I would be glad to. I want you to hold your hands together in your laps and close your eyes. Meditate on Amy Prescott, Jenna Jasmine, Rita Rocca, and Tessa Johnson's names. If you know them, concentrate on their essence. Go ahead, meditate. I'll guide you to step two in five minutes."

Just as before, I closed my eyes and concentrated on each woman. Fred hopped over and laid his head on my shoulder. Images of Tessa back on Watchtower came to mind. She was kind and deep and compassionate. She'd befriended me when I needed her. Rita was a spoiled woman who never grew up. The product of a second marriage after severe loss. She grew up with the drama of a missing older sister and a father grieving the murders of his first two children. Life for her couldn't have been easy.

Both Rita and Alinka thought they saw the missing daughter, Katlyn, in Moon Lake. Did the killer have Katlyn?

"Whoa, wait," I said.

"Faith, you're supposed to be quiet," Trixie said. "Now, we'll have to start over."

"But I've got another piece. I promise it's important. Hear me out."

"Go ahead, Faith," Sydney said. "The sooner we solve this, the sooner the guys let us out of prison."

"We are forgetting about Katlyn Johnson. Rita, seeing Katlyn, was what brought Alinka and Tessa into town. Does the killer have her?"

"You know, Rita asked me about Kat Carmichael the other day," Elle said. "She owns Moon Lake Pizza. I told Rita what I knew about Kat, but Kat doesn't socialize much. She'll come to a chamber of commerce meeting or town hall if it affects her business, but she keeps to herself."

"Where does she live?"

"Out on Jupiter Road, where there used to be that big red barn on the corner. Oh, shoot." Monique slapped her temple. "What if we saw the big red barn because that's how we'd recognize the property? Instead, we all interrupted it as we needed to look for a big red barn. Darn. I should have caught that."

Trixie tapped a pen on a hospital tray. "Ladies, before we send people chasing out there, let's get back to the crystal balls and see what additional information we can find. We don't have time to waste. Close your eyes and meditate."

We did. And this time, my mind allowed me to remain calm.

"Now put whichever hands speak to you on the ball, focus on your third eye, and gaze into the ball using that eye."

It was easier this time. I found my third eye faster. The ball grew warm in my hand, and the smoke inside swirled rapidly. I saw them tied to a post again, but the barn fell away to reveal a shed—one of those that look like log cabins.

"Open your eyes and tell me what you see."

"Is there a log cabin where that barn used to be?" I asked.

"Yes," Sydney said. "I only saw Kat in the cabin, not the others."

"Me too," said Tiffany.

"Okay," Vito said. "We'll send the guys."

Trixie tapped her pen again. "Ladies, you aren't done. Get back to your balls. If you only saw one person in the cabin, we have the rest to find."

"This stinks being stuck inside while the guys get to have the fun," Elle said.

"I hear you. I've gotten used to being in on the takedown," I said.

"Ladies, back to your balls," Trixie repeated. "You have important work to do."

"Yes, Mother."

"See, I got you to call me Mother again. Pretty soon, it will roll right off your tongue. We're going to try this another way," Trixie said. "Gaze into your balls, and I will ask you questions. Tell me the first thing you think of or see. If you don't know, say I don't know."

"Fire away, Mrs. Bracken," Sydney said.

"Where are the other girls?"

"I don't know," we chorused.

"Where is Tessa?"

Again, "I don't know was the answer."

"Where is Jenna?"

"In an old church," Tiffany said.

"What church?"

"Oh, Goodness. Right under our noses. The one up on the ridge. We'll go get her," Elle said, pushing herself away from the ball.

"Wait, it could be a trap," Tiff warned.

"We have ways," Elle said. "Monique and Lois, you stay here. Syd, Grace, and I will get her. We have ways."

"But," Tiff interrupted.

My heart raced.

"Don't worry," Monique said as the door shut behind her. "I borrowed some of The Alchemists Dust. They'll be fine. My cousins and aunt can shoot a flea off a man's nose, and they each have unique magical powers."

Blake knocked on the door and opened it. "Just making sure no one has escaped protective custody."

"We're still here, as you can see."

He looked from Tiffany to me and then to Monique.

"Where are the other two?"

"They needed a quick break. They sense things differently. Not used to crystal ball gazing." He looked at Tiffany.

"Okay, carry on." And then pulled his phone from his pocket as he rolled from the room.

"He is so calling Pete and Link."

"Yeah, I expect them to be knocking down the door any minute."

"Trixie, carry on with the next round before the guys arrive. And don't worry, Tiffany. If Jenna is in the church, we'll get her."

"Okay, where is Rita?" Trixie asked.

"Don't know." We responded.

"Where is Amy?"

"With Tessa and Rita," I said.

"Where are they?"

"Don't know."

"What do the surroundings look like?"

"Don't know."

"What do they smell?"

"Fruit," I said. "It smells like fruit."

"Molasses," said Monique.

"I smell bread," Tiff answered.

"Are you inside or outside?" Trixie asked.

"Inside a thin narrow building like the Willis tower but skinner and dustier."

"The old grain elevator," Monique said.

"I saw Rita on the ground holding her chest. Rita is sick. She can't wait. I'm going after her. And I'll bring her back. Tiff, call an ambulance. I said."

"Wait, I'm coming with you," Tiff said. "Grams, Monique, send an ambulance to the house."

"Tiff grabbed my hand, and we stepped into the In-Between." In the distance, I heard Vito yelling at Fred. I pictured the old grain elevator and took a step. When my left foot was fully planted on the elevator's dirt floor, I pulled my right foot to it. Tiffany was right beside me. On the floor lay Rita. Tessa and Amy struggled to reach her.

"Faith, oh, thank goodness. Rita has asthma. All this dust. She can't breathe." Tiffany was already working on Tessa's restraints. I started on Amy's. In a moment, we had them both freed from the posts.

"Help us get her up," Tiffany ordered. Tiff and I pulled Rita up and slipped her arms over our shoulders. Tessa held her from the front, and Amy clasped her hand from the back.

"Hold on, everyone, and believe." Tiffany sprinkled magic dust over us, which made Rita breathe harder. "Ivan," she yelled, and we snapped our fingers twice. This time, we again took a wild ride. We flipped, flopped, twisted, somersaulted, and finally came to land on the floor in front of Blake.

Paramedics banged on the door. When I opened the door, Harvey's men were gone, as were the sheriff's deputies.

As I stepped aside to allow the paramedics to enter, I looked at Blake. "Where did Harvey's men go?"

"I don't know. We sent cars to the Log Cabin. Pete, Arie, and Link are headed to the church on The Collins Spread. Vito's men are outside."

"Arie and I will yell at you later. First, I need to ask some questions. Of Tessa and Amy."

I helped Tessa and Amy into chairs and gave them a water bottle. "Tessa, did Upton do this to you?" I asked before Blake got the chance to talk. Confusion crossed her face.

"No, it wasn't Upton. It was one man. He wore a black ski mask. I had just entered my room at the inn. I sensed someone behind me. Before I could turn around, something sharp poked my neck, and I was out. I woke up in the elevator beside Rita. She had her inhaler in her pocket, but it gave out hours ago."

"Amy, did you see him?"

Amy wiped tears from her eyes and gulped water from the bottle. "No, like Tessa, I felt a sharp pain and woke up in the elevator the day before Tessa and Rita arrived. The kidnapper never spoke. He wore a ski mask, gloves, and a black windbreaker. He held a water bottle so I could drink, and he fed me a protein bar. He carries two phones. I saw them under his jacket when he got me a chair."

"Was he tall or short?"

"Tall, about your friend's height," Tessa said, inclining her head toward Blake.

"He must be older because I heard 'Gramps, pick up the phone' when his phone rang. It repeated several times," Amy added.

"Tessa, did Upton have children?"

Tessa rolled her eyes. "No, and there is no way in the universe he would have a phone ring. 'Gramps, pick up the phone.' It just wouldn't."

She was right. Not Upton's style.

"Did you get the sense he was the boss or a henchman?" Blake asked.

"The boss." Both women said.

"What made you say that?"

Tessa took a long sip of water. "He moved with confidence. He knew what he was doing. Someone who'd been in these situations before. He wasn't aggressive, but he wasn't pleasant. Sort of like a cop."

"Yeah, the way he moved with the jeans and boots, he could have played a western sheriff on an old TV show. He didn't seem like someone taking orders," Amy said.

"Tessa, after I left The Bahamas, did Special Agent Harvey Wallbanger come around regarding Brandon's death?"

"Yes, but they'd already caught the killer, and the Mask was returned. "

"Who was it?"

"The Pastor. He was a fake and an art thief."

Blake's phone rang. "Jenna is with me," Arie said through Blake's phone speaker. "There were signs of a struggle at the cabin, but we don't have Kat. Elle and Sydney are getting their butts chewed by Pete and Link, and then the ladies will return to protective custody. I'm headed back with Jenna."

"Arie, don't come here. Take Jenna to the Collins Spread with Pete and Link."

"What? Why?"

"Because he's waiting for you?"

"Who is waiting for me?"

"I don't know. I think it's Harvey, but something isn't right. Don't come back here. We have Vito's men, who have more magical training than you. Please, I beg you, don't go into the In-Between because Upton may be waiting."

"I don't like it," Arie said. "My daughter is there."

"Sorry, Bro, your daughter is a magic pro. Do you want her to have to rescue you? That's what will happen if you come here."

He huffed. "Alright. We'll stay on The Collins Spread."

"The paramedic came over to Tessa. Your sister is going to be fine. Her breathing should return to normal soon. We want to take her to the hospital, but she's refusing treatment. It sounds like a lot is going on here."

Tessa looked at Rita. "I think she needs to stay here. We'll get her into a doctor soon."

"Okay, thank you, Ma'am, and good luck."

He and his partner walked out the door.

Blake sat on the chair by Rita. "Rita, don't talk, just nod. Is Kat Carmichael of Moon Lake Pizza, your sister?"

"Yes, I'm sure it was Katlyn. I could tell the minute we saw each other. She recognized me too."

"But she didn't acknowledge you."

"No," Rita shook her head and used the inhaler the paramedics had given her.

"You know, that could be awkwardness. I sneaked into Abra a few times and didn't connect with Arie. I didn't want to do the drama. It was easier not to."

"Can we ask what is going on?" Tessa asked. "Why were we grabbed?"

Amy interrupted her. "After he grabbed me, I woke up in the car for a second. The kidnapper was talking to someone on the phone. Something about I was going to the highest bidder. At the time, I thought I was dreaming. I'm mean, I'm old and fat. Not exactly who I think of in human trafficking." She accepted a sandwich Tiffany made for her and Tessa.

"Please tell us what happened, and is Alinka okay?" Tessa pleaded.

My heart went out to her. She had to be terrified. She'd lived in the shadow of her two murdered older siblings. Tessa's mother committed suicide. Katlyn ran away. She and Rita had been kidnapped, and Tessa watched Rita almost die.

And then we needed to tell her about Alinka, her cousin, who was raised as her sister.

"Alinka is in the hospital," Blake said. "She fought her attacker and must have played dead. He dumped her body, but she was found and is in the hospital. She's critical but stable."

"Is all this because of that stupid mask? If so, they can have it."

"It was stolen again," I told her.

Tessa's lips and chin trembled. "My dad, Max, are they okay? Max was supposed to meet me."

"Yes, Max found me and asked me to help find you."

"Your father is on a plane headed here as we speak," Blake told Tessa.

"Can I see Max?"

"As soon as we figure this all out," Blake said. "Right now, the less contact you have with the outside world, the better."

My phone rang. It was Blister.

"This is Faith."

"Too important for our normal dance. Remember that phone in The Bahamas Max and Able called?"

"Yes."

"Max, Able, and three other phones are connected to it right now. And the phone isn't in the Bahamas. The phone is less than a quarter of a mile south of you in a wooded area off the road. Are there woods behind your house?"

"Yes,"

"Just one phone," Blake asked through the speaker.

"Just one."

Rita gasped for breath. Smoke poured in under the door. I looked out of the widow. Smoke filled the front porch.

Anger like I'd never experienced before raged through me.

"Get on the floor and crawl towards the back of the house," Blake ordered. "Get your noses to the space under the doors." The dogs who'd gone outside barked and ran from the fence to the doors and scratched. Harvey hadn't better touch a hair on any of their furry heads.

I couldn't contain the anger any longer. I grabbed hold of Fred, and we crawled to the French doors, where I cracked it just a bit.

"I call upon the Mask of Bluedorf." It appeared in my hand. "I seek the Dust of the Alchemist." A rainbow of twinkling magic floated above my head. "Capture the smoke within this house and surround the one who does us harm. I ask of thee now."

Nothing happened for a couple of seconds. Then the rainbow began to mix with the smoke.

The mask burst into flames of light. Smoke began to rise a few inches from the floor.

A whoosh crescendoed. The house shook.

The dust and smoke mixture rushed toward the back of the house. I had the sensation of the structure tipping backward.

In response, I opened the French door all the way. The twinkling, rainbow-colored smoke whirled and twisted into a tornado and raced across the backyard, tossing Sampson's obstacles here and there. The pup would never forgive me.

Harvey screamed. All that was visible were his feet twirling higher and higher. The tornado changed direction, coming back toward the house. Vito's men were now in the backyard. Harvey dropped from the sky and landed face first in a pile of dog poop.

Two of Vito's men grabbed him and zip-tied him, but left his face where it landed. Tiffany and I jumped off the deck and marched toward him. "Why?"

He struggled to sit. One of Vito's men wiped his face.

Harvey wept. "My ten-year-old grandson is sick. He suffers from a family genetic defect that causes a rare disease. It's so rare; the medicine is exorbitant and not covered under insurance.

"The only cure is a treatment which requires a brain surgeon and a Lighter Healer. I am of the Murker's lineage. Without the medicine or cure, my grandson won't see his eleventh birthday."

My insides churned. I wanted to hate this man. He'd murdered and abducted people and scared the life of everyone. Yet my heart ached for his grandson.

"Why didn't you just ask?"

"Because even if I found Lighter healers willing to work on him, I didn't have the money for the surgery."

"So what's that got to do with us?" I asked.

"Somehow, Upton's business partner figured out I was a Murker, and he knew about my grandson's medical problems. In exchange for losing a key piece of evidence, he told me the legend of The Lighter's Wand. Said his wife had been searching for it, but she'd been unable to find it."

"And then what happened?" Blake asked.

"We struck a deal. His wife is a Lighter Healer. If I found the wand and the Lighter Seventh Generation, she'd perform the healing, and he'd give me the money for the surgery."

"So Upton was never a part."

"A few days after we struck a deal, I was contacted by Upton Crescent, and a couple of days later, Max Peterson called. Three days later, a man I know only as the Researcher met me in the Bahamas. Each outbid the other."

"Why did you kill all those people?"

"I'm not saying another word. Right now, all you can prove is smoke bombs and tampering with evidence."

Tiffany walked up to Harvey, who still sat on the ground with his hand behind his back, and kicked him.

"Where is Kat Carmichael?"

"I've had no contact with Kat Charmichael. That's the truth."

Vito stomped into the backyard. "You give us the wand, and we heal your grandson. You give up your badge, and my organization detains you for twenty years."

"You find a surgeon and a healer, and I'll talk."

"I need his phone," Vito said. Stash reached into Harvey's pockets and retrieved two phones.

"Which of these gets me the boy's mother?"

"The flip."

"What's her name?"

"Bethany."

Vito opened the phone and flipped through the contacts. He put it near Harvey's face. "Tell her to have him here next Monday at noon."

When Harvey finished talking to his hope-filled daughter, Vito took back the phone.

"My word is golden. I need the location of the wand now. If I don't get it in the next few seconds, our deal is off, and you're going to prison for a very long time. We'll find the evidence we need."

Silence blanketed the yard. The dogs didn't move. Everyone held their breath. I found myself counting the seconds. We were up to ten Mississippis.

"I'd had it with me for months, but a few days ago, I placed The Lighter's Wand inside The Rabbit's Statue. I pried off the end cap and put it inside. When I did, I believe I freed Lester Cane's soul. He laughed so loud the factory shook."

"So he's back," Vito said.

# CHAPTER 28

One week later.

Since I'd learned about the Murks those first few days after returning to Abracadabra, I assumed that once we caught the serial killer, the Murks would be defeated, the curse reversed, and we could move on with our lives. Not so. But now, we had more tools to fight them. Unfortunately, the spirit of Lester Crane was on the loose.

Vito and his contacts retrieved the wand and secured it some place known only to them. Moon Lake Pizza had not reopened, and Kat Carmichael appeared to be in the wind.

Upton, Max, The Researcher, and Kat were still on the loose, and I suspected we weren't through with them yet.

Right now, Vito, Arie, Tiffany, Blake, Harvey, Harvey's daughter, and I sat deep within the secret bowels of the Magic Factory.

Trixie, Alinka, Ghost-Spirit Lily Collins, and Hekka from the Allegro Islands worked their magic healing powers while Trixie's surgical team operated on Harvey's grandson. How Vito persuaded Trixie's surgeon to operate remained a mystery.

The surgeon exited the operating room, followed by Trixie, Alinka, and Hekka. "He's going to be fine," the surgeon said.

Trixie smirked. "We make a good team, Doc."

# CHAPTER 29

Three Weeks Later.

I looked at my watch. In fifteen minutes, Abracadabra Magic Factory would open its door for a test run. A few family members and friends had been invited.

Vito came from the back of the building.

"Any evidence Lester Crane or Upton are around?"

"The only evidence I have is my gut. And my gut is shaking."

Five minutes to go. Two cars pulled into the parking lot, along with a floral delivery truck from a florist in South Bend. The driver opened the side door and brought out a massive vase with three dozen multi-colored Calla Lilies. Vito opened the door, and the driver placed the vase on the table.

"I need a signature," she said.

"Who are they for?" Vito asked.

"They are beautiful." I opened the card.

"Faith, we aren't done."

The End

**Find out what happens next.**

The Magic Factory is open for business and full of mystery, magic, and murder. *Mums, Magic, & Murder* is coming May 2025.

**A Note From Lucia**

Hi, Thank You for reading *Calla Lilies, Curses, & Criminals*. I do hope you enjoyed this book. Writing the magic scenes and spells is always a blast. And I so love to write about talking animals.

My cat, Xena, doesn't speak in words, but she lets me know what it is she wants. Often loudly and in the middle of the night.

This book was fun for me to write because it brought in the Collins Trio from my Moon Lake Series. Jenna Jasmine from my Psychic Cat Series, and Alyssa and Hekka,

the Bumbling Witch from The Ghosts of The Allegro
Islands Series.

I'd love to connect with you. All of my contact information is on my website at LuciaKuhl.Com.

May you have a wonderful day!

Lucia

．

### Series by Lucia Kuhl

The Magic in Moon Lake Series
The Flower Farm Series
The Psychic Cat Series
The Ghosts of The Allegro Islands Series
The Mystwood Retreats Series @ Moon Lake
The Willow's Creek Murder Club Series
The Pair-A-Dice Psychic Sleuths Series

Coming Soon Cozy Mystery Series:
Glimmerton Paranormal Powers Series
Haunted Homestead Series

Made in United States
Cleveland, OH
28 September 2025